The Secrets of Brysons Grove

The Secrets of Brysons Grove

JW AMBROSE

Primix Publishing
East Brunswick Office Evolution
1 Tower Center Boulevard, Ste 1510
East Brunswick, NJ 08816
www.primixpublishing.com
Phone: 1-800-538-5788

© 2025 JW ambrose. All rights reserved.

No part of this book may be reproduced, stored in a retrieval system, or transmitted by any means without the written permission of the author.

Published by Primix Publishing: 08/01/2025

ISBN: 979-8-89194-484-8(sc)
ISBN: 979-8-89194-485-5(e)

Library of Congress Control Number: 2025909855

Any people depicted in stock imagery provided by iStock are models, and such images are being used for illustrative purposes only.

Certain stock imagery © iStock.

Because of the dynamic nature of the Internet, any web addresses or links contained in this book may have changed since publication and may no longer be valid. The views expressed in this work are solely those of the author and do not necessarily reflect the views of the publisher, and the publisher hereby disclaims any responsibility for them.

Introduction

T he wind was rustling the hanging plants on the front porch of the old antebellum home. You could smell the aroma of the fried chicken slowly drifting through the windows. Standing on the porch, he watched the smoke curl from the cigar. Thoughts of times and people gone by haunted him. Miss. Charlotte sure was good in the kitchen. Side dishes of green beans and mashed potatoes with home brewed tea would be the flavor of the night. The moon shone brightly through the trees. The chill in the air was almost eerie as he thought back to the events that had taken place just a year ago.

His divorce had been one of the most challenging events of his life. Although it was agreeable to both parties, it still lingered in his thoughts more than he would like to admit. Patricia, his ex wife, had long since moved away, but the memories still lingered. *"Oh* well," he thought as he made his way into the kitchen, "better start gathering up some more firewood, the chill in the air just means that fall is here, and winter won't be far behind."

Chapter One

Crossing the bridge over Stinson's Creek, the fog rose slowly from the surface of the water. Six miles to the office, the same route every day to work, and luckily a different way home. Being a land surveyor for the state was sometimes boring, but there was always the surprise of finding something that had been discarded long ago, or simply something that someone had tried to hide. Cold cereal for breakfast had given way to the frozen biscuits he bought at the grocery store last week. Juggling the last cup of coffee in his travel mug and driving was his regular morning routine. As he passed the turn off at Preacher's Fork, he noticed the same eight-point buck that grazes in the walnut grove near the creek. Amazing how he gets around in the area. He had seen him up close once from the cross hairs of his hunting rifle, but just could not seem to pull the trigger. Something about the way that old fellow looked at him, as if to let him know that he knew he was watching and wondering if it was going to be his last meal. Since then, every time he had seen him grazing, he thought about the look that old deer had given him.

Not much happening in Bryson's Grove this morning. Just the usual clamber down Main Street, the travelers in the kitchen at Charlotte Parker's bed and breakfast were sipping the coffee and savoring the smell of the muffins that she had baked for them. Although she was only in her early forties, she had quite a reputation for the good cook and hostess that she was. Most of the visitors to Bryson's Grove had learned of her establishment by word of mouth, and the scenery in the hills of Eastern Tennessee is breathtaking this time of the year. She had only advertised in the Knoxville Journal twice since she had moved back to this sleepy little town after her mother died, and she had often wondered what it would have been like if she advertised more. There wasn't a weekend in the fall that she wasn't busy. She had to start taking reservations a year in advance in order to make sure she could accommodate the people who visited for the fall colors. Her career as a designer of women's clothes in New York had gotten to be almost more than she could handle. The deadlines, color and fashion selections, and the general hustle and bustle of the city were beginning to bear on her sanity. Now she could at least get away from "Charlotte's Manor", (what she lovingly called it although it didn't have an official name) whenever she wanted to even if it was only to spend the evening with Jake. Very few people in Bryson's Grove knew nothing about their relationship and she and Jake wanted to keep it that way.

Jake checked the fax machine and the voice mail on his phone to see if there were any assignments for the week. The weekend he had spent with Charlotte had been exciting as usual, and although he could handle the business from a remote location such as his home, he liked the idea of having an office in town so he would have someplace to go every day; plus it afforded him the opportunity to keep an eye and an ear on the happenings in town. Two phone calls for work and a voice mail from his parents in Florida were the only messages he had. He had a reasonable backlog of work as the opportunities from the state government kept him pretty busy, and being able to travel statewide, pretty well kept him on the go. As he packed his gear for the first assignment, he made a mental note to go by the post office to check the mail before he left. Picking up his daily copy of the Bryson Grove Sentinel, he headed over to Annie's Café for his second round of coffee. It was a treat to spend a little time over there reading the paper and having another cup of coffee. Also, it was a great way to catch up on the latest scuttlebutt on the townspeople. As he pulled out the chair of his favorite table by the window, Andrew Turner, the president of the bank, was being his loud and boisterous self. Talking about how his wife had gone shopping in the big city and how much money she had spent. Being twenty-five years his junior, she obviously had to find some form of entertainment because there wasn't much in this "little hick town," as she called it.

The shopping was just a cover up for the affair she was having with a friend who takes up for Andrew's deficiencies.

"Got your measuring stick out for today?"

Deputy Roger Pinson asked, as he pulled up a chair across from Jake's table.

"Yep, ready to go," was his reply.

Jake wasn't too fond of the Buford Pusser "want to be" that Roger portrayed. Although he wasn't threatened by the deputy, he thought that it would be better left alone that the deputy was an asshole most of the time, and that he preyed on the vacationers as they rumbled down the state highway just on the outskirts of town.

This was his cue to get to work. He didn't want to spend the rest of the morning listening to Roger tell about the exciting tickets he had written.

"Wonder if he has more than one bullet?" Jake laughed under his breath as he paid Sue Ellen for the coffee and walked out the door. He thought about the two-hour drive he had to take to get to the land he needed to survey for the Park Services." *If only this old truck could talk, what tales it could tell."*

It had been a gift from his father after he made the football team in high school, and even though it had over 100,000 miles on it, it still got him around. Besides, he just couldn't part with it because of the memories of all the panties he had hidden under the seat just in case his mother came out and looked in it after a Friday night on the town after a football game. Little did he know that his mother had long since found the journal that Jake kept about all of the things that were happening to him in his senior year. Although it didn't make the best sellers list of any of the three Publishers he sent it to, he figured it must have given them a good laugh anyway. As he reached in the CD case for his favorite Eagles album, he noticed the package lying on the passenger seat. He could recognize that smell anywhere. The fresh baked muffins would be a welcome treat about seventy-five miles down the road. He had forgotten that he told Charlotte that he would be away from town till tomorrow, and apparently she had made the snack for him earlier. As he pulled out onto highway 70 he turned the volume up louder and his thoughts drifted again to what he had found a year ago.

He fumbled with the key to the lockbox on the key chain as he switched over into the left lane to pass Joe Murphy's hay bailer.

"One of these days I'm going to find out what is in there," he thought, *" but not today."*

The Brewster County engineer was right on time. The maps and legends he had were a few years old, but they would be sufficient. They were at least enough to help Jake get the information and make the measurements that he needed. They needed measurements on the north end of the park in order to make some improvements to the camping areas. As he set up his instrument, he had to kick a few Budweiser cans out of the way. *"Looks like the kids had one hell of a party here last night," he thought as he set the level. This would only take a couple of hours, and if he hurried, he might make it back by bedtime.*

Little did he know that beer cans weren't all that he would find.

As he moved to another section of the area behind a fire pit, he noticed what he thought was a pair of shoes on the ground. As he got closer he realized that they weren't only shoes, there was someone there. As he made his way to the back of the fire pit, he saw that a young woman was lying on the ground. He checked for a pulse and there was none. Realizing that she was dead, he hurried down to the service road where his truck was parked and looked for his cell phone. There was no service in this remote area. He started up his truck and sped towards the ranger's residence. He was almost out of breath as he ran up the walkway to the porch.

"What in the hell happened to you?" the ranger said.

"You look like you have seen a ghost!"

"There is a body behind the fire pit!" Jake said.

With that, the ranger grabbed his hat and gun and followed Jake back to the site. Sure enough, there was a body there. There was no identification around anywhere, and the cause of death could not be immediately determined. It wasn't long before the local authorities arrived and an investigator from the Federal Marshall's office. Because the body was found on government property, the Federal Marshall was in charge of the investigation. After taking Jake's statement, and finding out that he wasn't from there locally, they asked him to stay overnight as they wanted to question him some more in the morning. He had to stay anyway; he had to finish the job he was sent to do.

"The survey will have to be done at another time", the ranger said.

"It will take two or three days to comb the area for clues."

"Son of a bitch," Jake thought.

"Looks like a two day assignment is going to turn into another damned fiasco!"

The ranger offered to let him stay at the park residence, but Jake refused, saying that he would just get a room at one of the local motels near the park. One of the last things the Marshall asked him was if he had touched the body or any of the articles in the immediate area. Jake's reply was to the negative, and they let him go. They wanted to confiscate his equipment, but after realizing that wouldn't happen without a fight, they decided to let Jake take it with him. There was something uncannily familiar about Jake, the marshal thought but he just couldn't put his finger on it; he would find out later what it was.

The only motel in town didn't have a lounge; it almost didn't have any rooms. There were so many people in the mountains this time of the year; you almost had to drag a tent and a sleeping bag around with you for the month of October and November. Luckily there was a small local beer joint not too far from the motel, and Jake decided to go there for a cold beer. There wasn't anything else to do in this town, the park was the main attraction for at least fifty miles, and he wasn't in the mood to go traveling around just looking for a drink. He had a bottle of his favorite Canadian Reserve in the truck, but he wasn't about to get that out. Besides, beer would help him to sleep better, or at least he thought it would. He sat down at the bar, and he hadn't much more than got his drink, when an old man sat down beside him and said,

"You that photographer feller that was walking around in the park and found the body?"

"That would be me," Jake said, "but I ain't no photographer, I am a surveyor."

"Makes no difference," the old man said, "word sure gets around pretty fast here!"

As it does in most small towns," Jake thought.

"What do you reckon happened to her," the bartender asked.

"I don't know," Jake replied

"All I saw was the body and I hightailed it to the ranger's residence to let them know."

By this time most of the five or six other customers in the bar were gathered around Jake like he was preaching the gospel or something. Not much happens in this small town, and Jake was glad he didn't live anywhere near here. He almost had second thoughts about going inside anyway, all the pick-up trucks outside had rebel flag license plates on the front of them, not to mention that they were all backed into the parking places as if to give them a quick getaway. After finishing his beer, he walked outside to his truck. As he pulled out of the parking lot, he noticed the black sedan sitting across the street. As he drove by it he recognized the driver as the federal Marshall who had questioned him. The Marshall followed him back to the motel, and as Jake pulled in, the Marshall kept going.

"Wonder what the hell he wants?" Jake thought as he entered the room. As he opened the door, the Marshall's business card had been shoved under the door. Jake didn't know if he was given a second one on purpose, or if the officer had forgotten that he had given Jake one at the scene of the crime. Jake laid it on the table. As he took off his shoes and turned the television on, he had just got there in time for the local news. There he was, "big as life and twice as ugly." He thought.

"This is all I need! Oh well, maybe it will be good for business,"

He laughed under his breath. But in reality he knew that it was only the beginning of a nuisance for him. The last thing he wanted was to have him plastered all over the television. He had started the surveying business to get away from the people and the crowds, not to have reporters and the news media all over him. He turned off the television and got ready for bed. As usual the mattress felt like the top of a pool table. Not a comfortable place to sleep, but if you are too drunk to drive at Mert's Tavern in Bryson's Grove, that is the only place to sleep it off. Luckily for him, he was where he didn't have to worry about the law bothering him, or at least he thought, anyway.

The Marshall took another sip of his coffee and adjusted the steering wheel. He had requested some additional information on Jake Stuart and unless the answers came back wrong, he would be there most of the night.

Annie's was closing for the night when the news came on. There he was, Jake Stuart, local businessman from Bryson's Grove on national television. Charlotte had been in for a glass of tea, and was just leaving as the news came on. She could see the disgust in Jake's eyes as the cameras were right in his face as the reporters questioned him. All they knew was that Jake had found the body while doing some survey work and that the young woman had only been dead for a few hours. There had been some fingerprints lifted from some beer cans found near the body, but that was all the information that the authorities were giving out at this time. Charlotte excused herself and went home. She put the tea on the table and tried to reach Jake on his cell phone. It went immediately to voice mail. There had been one phone call on her caller I D but it was listed as an out-of –area call. She wondered if the call was his. She went upstairs to get ready for bed and as she laid her keys on the nightstand, she looked at the key to Jake's house and remembered the last time she was there. His denim shirt still had a whiff of his cologne on it, for some reason she was really missing him. She wondered if it was because she knew that he was troubled about all of this or if she just wanted to be close to him again.

The sun shone through the opening in the curtains and Jake watched for a while as it creeped up the wall. He had been awake for some time, hell; he didn't sleep for most of the night. He had chalked it up to a difference in the mattress of the motel but deep down inside of him he knew that wasn't the only reason. It had been a long time since he had been so close to a corpse and it wasn't a good feeling. After taking a shower, he headed towards the restaurant for some coffee and breakfast. The ranger was already there and so was the Marshal. They had just sat down as Jake was entering the building.

"Come on over and join us," was the ranger's reply, "we were just about to come and get you."

There was no further information on the girl. There wasn't any identification found anywhere, and they had to send the body to Knoxville because that was the nearest forensic service. The Marshal went over the same questions that he had asked the day before, and Jake gave him the same answers. "I will continue my investigation and will probably be contacting you in Bryson's Grove." He spoke.

"As soon as we find out who she is, we will have to determine where she was from and what she was doing there. I will need you to go with me to the sheriff's office so I can get your fingerprints."

Jake knew that the Marshal wasn't really interested

in his fingerprints to compare them to the beer cans; he wanted them to see if Jake had a record. Although he had never been arrested, his fingerprints were on file with the federal government as he had been in the Special Forces during his time in the service.

The ranger finished his breakfast and left Jake and the Marshal at the table.

"Just what do you want to know about me?" Jake asked as the Marshal took another sip of coffee.

"I know you from somewhere, and I am just trying to place you." He said. Jake knew that unless the Marshal was from around Bryson's Grove that he was lying. He had lived there for the last ten years after coming home from the service, and had agreed to keep the family home up after his parents retired to Florida, and he had never seen the Marshal before yesterday. They left the restaurant and walked down the street to the sheriff's office. Jake gave another statement and they fingerprinted him.

"Were you ever in the service?" the Marshal asked.

"I am sure by now that you know that I was in the Green Berets," Jake told him.

"I am not dumb enough to think that you haven't already ran my social security number and driver's license just to see what you could find."

"Ever been in any trouble?" he said with a commanding voice.

"Not anything that I couldn't get myself out of." Jake replied.

About that time, the fax machine buzzed and the

report from Knoxville came through. The girl was Martha Ann Sawyer from Knoxville, TN. She was 22 years old and had been missing from home for two days. The last time she had been seen was with some of her friends at a local convenience store on the edge of town. The cause of death was due to an overdose of alcohol. Her blood alcohol test had come back at 27%. She had a medical history of heart trouble, and the alcohol had been the "poison" that she didn't need. Her parents had been contacted and were on the way to the police station in Knoxville. The Marshal would have to meet them there to interview them also.

"Looks like you aren't needed anymore, son." The Marshal said. Jake thanked him and walked out the door. Somehow, he had a gut feeling that he hadn't seen the last of him. As he got back to the park, the ranger allowed him back into the area where the girl was found so he could finish his assignment. They were in another area trying to find any clues as to who could have been there with the girl. The fingerprints from the beer cans were inconclusive and would have to be analyzed further. As Jake finished his measurements, the ranger thanked him for his help and told him he could leave anytime he was ready.

The drive back home was somewhat uncomfortable, as he couldn't figure out why the Marshal had been hounding him so much. He had no contact with the government since his discharge, and his records were as clean as Charlotte's kitchen. Speaking of Charlotte, he should make a phone call and see if she would be available for dinner tonight.

The phone rang, and as she reached for the receiver, she had a strange feeling that it would be him. When she recognized the number she didn't say hello, she just said,

"I would like to get in line for an autograph. I don't know many celebrities, and an autographed picture of the star witness would look good in the living room."

"Thanks a lot", was his reply, "I'll try to make some time for you about sevenish this evening."

"That's about the time I was thinking of myself, see you then." As she hung up the phone she felt a warm sensation about her. She would be packing an overnight bag.

He pulled onto the open road and turned the radio up a little louder. He smiled, as he knew he was in for an exciting time. The trip home seemed somewhat shorter than the original one, guess it was because he had so much on his mind.

As he pulled into the garage, he noticed that she was already there. Glancing at his watch it was a little before seven. As he walked through the living room, he caught a glimpse of a beautiful pair of legs just below the tail of his shirt. As she turned around he also saw that it was only buttoned half way. She walked toward him with the grace of a feline on the prowl. As she handed him the bottle of beer, she slowly and passionately kissed him on the lips. "Welcome home," she said.

"I have been looking forward to seeing you tonight."

"Me too," he said. "Sure made the drive home worth it."

He sat the bottle on the table and held her ever so gently. As he kissed her, she had to stand on her toes to reach him. His soft touch on her backside sent shivers up her spine. That coupled with the kisses, sent her into orbit. His kisses were one of the things she liked most about Jake. She had been intimate with him several times and the kisses were the thing that excited her the most. He slowly lifted her into his arms and walked toward the bedroom. "Dinner will get cold," she said.

"Damn the bad luck," he smiled and said. "Guess we will just have to warm it up." She had already made a fire in the bedroom fireplace and the flames had a seductive glow about them. As he laid her gently on the bed, he excused himself for a shower. "I need to get the road grime off me, be back in a minute." He said as he started undressing and walked toward the bathroom. As he turned the hot water up she opened the shower door and stepped in.

"I need another one myself, all of that cooking made me hot and sweaty."

He let the hot water tickle them ever so gently and traced the lines of her body with his strong hands; another one of his attributes. As they found a tender place, she gasped for breath. He slowly lifted her into his arms again and made love to her passionately. Over and over again the sensations traveled deeper into her body.

Toweling each other dry was another experience. She moved very seductively across the room and motioned him over to the bed. Their eyes met as he looked down at her sitting on the side of the bed. The last thing he remembered before he turned out the light was her gentle touch and kisses. Sometime in the middle of the night the warm glow of the fireplace embers mesmerized her as she fell asleep in his arms. They had stopped long enough to snack on the dinner she had prepared and she had stored the rest of the food in the refrigerator for another day.

He kissed her goodbye on the front porch.

"Aren't you going into town this morning?" she asked.

"No, I am going to take care of some things around here, and finish the assignment that I didn't get to yesterday." He said.

She thought that was strange, but passed it off to him being subjected to the events of yesterday. She got into her car and headed down the road. He lost sight of her as she rounded the bend in the road, and thought to himself, *"what a woman, sure is nice to have her around."*

By the time she had arrived in town, most of the early morning activities were already over. Her assistant in the boarding house had already made breakfast and the patrons were loading their cars and making arrangements to leave. She stopped by the post office to check her mail and ran into Diana Turner, the banker's wife. Charlotte tried her best to avoid her at all costs. She simply didn't like the way Diana looked at her each time they met somewhere. She had an eerie feeling that Diana was interested in her in a romantic kind of way, and she was not going to have any part of that. She had heard most of the rumors about Mrs. Turner's likening of women, and she wasn't interested in her at all. No one in town knew anything about her past before she and Andrew got married and she had often wondered if it wouldn't be a good idea for someone to check her out. She passed the time of day with her in the lobby and excused herself to "take care of some unfinished business." As she walked into the door of the bed and breakfast she had a flashback of some of the previous night's events and a warm feeling came over her. There was no doubt that she was in love with Jake, but that word had never been spoken between them. It had been the better part of two years since they had started seeing each other and she relished all the time she had spent with him. They had met at the fall festival in town shortly after she had moved back from New York. They already knew who each other was, but there had been no physical contact between them. They danced, ridden some of the carnival rides together and even shared one of those coneys that are ever so popular at the fair. The next week he had stopped by the bed and breakfast and asked her if she would like to go to the movies, and she reluctantly agreed. She had made herself a promise that she wasn't going to get involved with anyone else.

She had gone out to dinner with Deputy Pinson once, only because he had hounded her for two weeks; but that had been the extent of her social life in Bryson's Grove. But the situation with Jake was different. He was mysterious in an appealing sort of way. He had been a gentleman each time they were together. The first time they spent the night together was because she had offered to cook dinner for them at his home. The atmosphere in the old antebellum home reminded her of the Rhett Butler story, only on a smaller scale.

Jake was unusually organized for a single man living alone. He cleaned up after himself and everything was always put back into its place after it was used. She attributed this way of living because of his training in the service, or maybe from his parents. The high ceilings and the open floor plan gives a feeling of freedom, not the confining nature of most homes with small rooms and short ceilings. His kitchen was masculine but cozy. His parents had left most of their furniture and the old pots and pans and cooking utensils when they moved. It was almost like being at her grandmother's house all over again. She had so much fun; she couldn't believe she enjoyed it so much. She did that same thing so much at bed and breakfast. After their first dinner he had opened a bottle of wine and they sat on the front porch swing. He had reluctantly opened the humidor and took out one of his favorites, only to put it back.

"Light it up," she said. "I enjoy the smell of a good cigar."

She didn't know the difference between a good one and a bad one, but she figured that if he kept it in a humidor that it had to be better than the cigars that are sold in town that come five to a pack. Also, she knew that if they came in a round metal case, they must be primo. They sat there for a long time laughing and sipping the wine, talking about most anything that they could think of. She had wanted to kiss him again since that first night. His soft passionate kisses weren't the norm for a man of his stature, and she relished every one. She leaned over and kissed him gently; as he put his arms around her she knew she was in trouble. His soft but firm touch sent shivers up and down her spine. They stood and danced on the porch to the tune of Kenny G; and danced their way right into the house; all the way to the bedroom. She had no intentions of letting it go that far, but it had been so long for her that she threw caution to the wind and gave in. It was one of the most wonderful nights of her life.

The phone rang and she suddenly came back to reality. She had ordered some supplies from one of the local distributors in Knoxville, and they were calling to let her know that they were going to be another day late. Much to her dismay, she agreed to the delay, but her customers were not going to be happy that the stuffed olives were not going to be on the menu for a couple of days. She wondered what Jake was doing about this time, but she couldn't be concerned with that, she had work of her own to do.

Jake loaded up his camera and started out of the driveway. He had given up on the small surveying assignment that was in the works and thought that he would take some pictures. His hobby was photography and it was a stress relief for him. He had many black and white photographs that he had taken over the years, and even had some of them framed in his office. Several people had asked him where they came from, and he just passed them off as purchases from the craft store in the next town.

As he passed the walnut grove, there stood old "Grouchy." That was his name for the eight pointer that stood there some mornings and Jake would swear that that old buck was grunting at him. He stopped the truck and took out his telephoto lens and got a great shot of him standing under the trees. It was almost as if the deer knew what he was doing and was striking a pose for him. He headed down the road and at Preacher's Fork; he turned left instead of right and headed out into the country. The leaves were beginning to really show their colors, and he had promised Charlotte that he would make some pictures for her to put in the new brochure she was dreaming up for the bed and breakfast. He had once told her that she needed to think up a name for it, but she just blew him off and said that it was ok the way it was. As he topped the hill and started towards the old iron bridge over Sain's Creek, he noticed Deputy Pinson's patrol car sitting in the middle of the bridge with both doors open. He stopped his truck behind the car and as he walked to the driver's side, he saw a gruesome sight. Roger Pinson slumped over the steering wheel with a gunshot wound to the head. *"This is not good," he thought.*

"Two murders in one week are just almost more than I can stand."

He took out his cell phone and called Sheriff Thompson. The sheriff told Jake to stay put until he could get there. He had told Jake that he had been trying to get the deputy on the radio for a while, but to no avail. After what seemed to be an eternity, the sheriff and the local ambulance arrived. After a careful examination of the area, the coroner was called. It wasn't long after that the local office of the Tennessee Bureau of Investigation in Knoxville was called in to help with the investigation of the crime. A preliminary assessment by the coroner had placed the time of death around six a.m. The deputy always started work around 5 a.m. to catch some of the speeders on the main highway going to work in the paper mill just west of Bryson's Grove. A quick examination of his ticket book showed that he had written three speeding tickets that morning, but there was something unusual about the book. There were two consecutive copies missing out of the book as if someone had torn them out and threw the book on the ground. Jake was getting a little edgy. He knew that several people in town didn't like the deputy, but he never dreamed that anyone would be mad enough at him to do this. After an extensive interview with the authorities, they let Jake go and he headed towards town. The bridge and the road were closed for the rest of the day while bloodhounds were brought in to search the area, and even a helicopter came to their aid to help scour the area for clues. Nothing else was found but some tire tracks on the opposite end of the bridge going west to where Preacher's Fork connected back into Highway 70. The forensic officers made a plaster cast and pictures of the tire treads.

All the way to town Jake tried to think who could have done such a thing. When he got to town he stopped by the boarding house and told Charlotte what had happened. She told Jake that she had not seen the deputy in town all morning and was curious as to why he hadn't been to Annie's for his usual morning cup of coffee. They visited for a while and Jake walked over to his office to check for messages and faxes. It didn't take long for the news to spread around town. Jake stayed in the office most of the afternoon trying to catch up on paperwork and just get through the day. Later on, in the afternoon the sheriff came back to town and stopped by Jake's office. They went over his story again and everything seemed to be on the up and up. The sheriff went to his office to look over the deputy's ticket mail for the last few days. About an hour later he came back to Jake's office with some startling news. One of the tickets that the deputy had written two days before that was issued to Mary Ann Sawyer. Sheriff Thompson dropped the ticket on Jake's desk and said,

"Isn't this the girl that was found dead in the park yesterday?"

Much to his amazement, the sheriff was correct. She

was the victim found in the park. The sheriff produced the other ticket, and it had been issued to Paul Simpson, a worker at the paper mill. Obviously, who ever tore the tickets out of the book didn't think about the copies that had been turned in. Another good reason that the deputy's briefcase had been almost torn apart and all of the contents dumped into the front floorboard of the patrol car.

"Looks like the shooter was looking for these, doesn't it?" the sheriff asked.

He went back to his office and started looking for a telephone number for this man. According to the information on the citation, the only address for him was a post office box in Sevierville, which was just before you got to Knoxville. He ran the driver's license number on the NCIC machine, and it came back no record. Also there was no address for a Paul Simpson in any of the telephone books in the immediate area. The sheriff decided to go to the paper mill the next day and ask some questions. It was getting too late to drive over this evening, as the office would be closed and access to the employee records wouldn't be available. The sheriff phoned the TBI agent assigned to the investigation, and they agreed to meet at the sheriff's office the next morning. It was getting late and the agent, Jonathan Miller decided to stay in town for the night. The forensic guy had long since been gone and he had been talking to some of the townspeople about the deputy's activities. He opted to stay at Charlotte's bed and breakfast for the night instead of the fleabag hotel that he had passed on the way into town. According to the townspeople, she had better accommodation anyway, and the food was for damned sure better than the greasy spoon in the hotel. He knocked on the door and when she came to answer it he showed her his credentials and asked for a room for the night.

"You are lucky," she said. "I had someone check out just this morning and the other reservation won't be arriving until tomorrow afternoon."

"Thank you, mam," was his reply. "I will be leaving tomorrow myself."

She informed him that dinner was at six and that if he wanted to be sure to get some of her homemade apple pie, he better not be late. She showed him to his room and he asked for the use of a telephone. "There is one in the room here, and if you want to connect to the Internet, you will have to come downstairs. I have personal access myself, but I don't usually let anyone else use it. But in your case, I will make an exception if it will help you with your investigation."

"Do you know what happened out there today?" he asked.

"Not really," she replied.

"Just what the local gossip chain is passing out. Most of these old ladies in this town have better communications than you do," she laughed.

"I suppose you are probably right. I'll just be a minute on the phone and then I will need to finish my report."

"Take all the time you need," she said. "If you miss the apple pie, it will be your fault."

She retired upstairs to her personal quarters and called Jake on the phone.

"Are you alright?" She asked.

"About as well as can be expected given the circumstances." was his reply.

"There is something mighty funny about all of this, and I hope they get to the bottom of it soon."

Then he told her what the sheriff had found out and asked her if she had ever heard of a Paul Simpson. She replied no, that name didn't ring a bell. He told her that he was going home and would talk to her later. She invited him over for dinner but he declined.

Driving down the road the thought of the "book" that was in the lockbox at the bank and wondered if he should get it out and read some more of the entries in it.

Isaiah Bryson's journal had some interesting entries in it. Jake had found it in an old metal box just a year ago while he was surveying the Bryson family farm for the bank. He had started reading some of the information in it. Some of it was pretty damaging, but he stopped when he got to the part about Andrew Turner, his wife and the insurance lady all sleeping together in the same bed. It seemed that old Mr. Bryson had stopped by the banker's house one afternoon while the insurance lady was there and overheard some of the conversations about the previous night's activities. No one knew about the journal the old fellow kept, and rightly so, if they did it would make one hell of a television show. Also there was an old yellow envelope with someone's hand-written name on the front. . He just left it un opened and in the box. He figured the old man had enough turmoil in his life, and that the banker, the nephew, and the developers could just fight it out in court. They never could talk Mr. Bryson into agreeing to sell the family farm. It was one of the largest parcels in the county. Several developers had approached the old gentleman about buying it for a new housing development and he had declined. It seems that the paper mill was going to make a major expansion and the property would make an excellent development of middle-income homes for all of the people who would be coming to work there. Mr. Bryson just told them that he had all of the money he needed and that he just wasn't interested. Of course Andrew Turner had talked to some of the developers and secretly had been offered a "finder's fee" if he could talk the old man into selling the property. When he couldn't get the old man to sell, he called his only living relative, a nephew in Philadelphia, and had several meetings with him. The nephew had the old man committed as being insane and incompetent and the fight was on. Old Mr. Turner would have a fit if he knew that type of information was just under his nose.

Jake had known Isaiah Bryson all of his life. Many times after school he would stop by the old man's farm and fish in his pond. He even went over to help the old man in the wintertime store up firewood for the old pot-bellied stove that he used for heat. Right before

Jake left for his overseas assignment with the armed services, he stopped to tell the old man goodbye. His wife, Addie had just passed away and he wanted to give the old man his condolences. All through his tour of duty he kept up with the old man through his parents. He would even go by his house whenever he came in on furlough. When he was discharged from the service, he started helping the old man with his chores again. Mr. Bryson had passed away just a few months before Jake found the journal. Damned shame he thought as he pulled into the garage.

Jonathan Miller and sheriff Thompson had agreed to meet at the sheriff's office at 7 a.m. the next morning. As they drove out of town, they discussed the events leading up to the recent happenings. Agent Miller asked several questions about Jake and said that it was quite a coincidence that Jake would be the one to find both bodies. The sheriff agreed, but also said that he had known Jake and his family for many years. He told the agent about Jake being decorated for outstanding military service, and that the only time that he had been in trouble was when he staggered out of Mert's Tavern the day after his wife left him, too drunk to walk, much less drive. The sheriff admitted that he picked him up and took him to the jail to sleep it off so he wouldn't hurt himself. After a few more questions about the townspeople they made it to the paper mill. The manager, Charles Davis, was in a meeting with the department heads and it took a few minutes to get to the visitors. He checked the records for Paul Simpson and said that he didn't have a record of anyone ever working there by that name. Most of the employees were local and they and their families had been working there for a couple of generations.

The two officers thanked the manager and excused themselves. They would go back to town and wait for the reports on the fingerprints that were taken from the passenger side window of the deputy's patrol car. By the time they made it back to Bryson's Grove the forensic report had been faxed from Knoxville. It revealed that the fingerprints on the deputy's passenger side window matched those on one of the beer cans that were found at the scene of the crime in the park. They were in the process of running them through the F B I's fingerprint files in Washington to see if there was a match. The officer in charge of the forensic investigation advised that as soon as there was any new information at all, they would let him know.

Agent Miller thanked the sheriff for his help and gave him his condolences for the deputy. After viewing the deputy's personnel file, he left him his contact numbers and they agreed to talk again as soon as any new information is available.

Deputy Roger Pinson was single, and lived alone. His work was his life. He had moved to Bryson's Grove about ten years earlier from Sevierville where he had taken the test for police officer and failed it. He had decided to get away from the big cities to try living in a small town for a while. He had attended the local junior college and graduated from the criminology courses necessary for becoming a police officer, with flying colors. He answered the ad in the paper for the deputy's position and made the highest score on the test. The only other person to apply at the time was a relative of the manager at the paper mill, he left town after Roger Pinson was hired and no one ever heard from him again. While going through the deputy's personnel file, he came across the test scores. At this point he remembered the young man who had applied for the job and didn't get it. It took a while, but after digging through some old records, he came up with the application. Thank goodness he never threw anything away. This time he thought he had it. The applicant's name was Byron Davis. He relayed this information to Jonathan Miller and hoped for some results.

He stopped reading long enough to walk over to Annie's for a quick bite of food. It seemed like the whole town was in the restaurant and of course they all had the same questions to ask. He knew this was a mistake, so he just told Sue Ellen to make him a cheeseburger and he would go back to the office.

Damned nosy people anyway.

When he had reached his office, Jake was sitting in the chair across from the Sheriff's.

"I don't guess you have found anything yet, have you?"

Jake asked with a concerned look on his face.

"Not really, have been most of the morning looking for some old information." He replied.

"Anything interesting?" Jake asked.

"Not really, and if I had found something, you know I couldn't tell you. Hell, they still haven't counted you out as one of the suspects. Not too many people find two dead bodies in the same week. Jake, I know you didn't kill Roger, and I know you didn't have anything to do with the young girl from Knoxville, but convincing the state authorities is going to be another chore. Now get your ass out of here and let me eat before this dam hamburger gets cold!" The sheriff said with a grin.

"If I need to talk to you about anything, I'll get in touch with you even if I have to drive out to your place."

"Thanks, I'll see you later," Jake said as he walked out the door.

As he walked back to his office, he thought about taking off for a couple of days. He nixed that idea because he thought if he did, the authorities would be even more suspicious of him. When he opened the door, the fax machine was humming.

Good, he thought, another assignment. Maybe he could use the time to take his mind of the events of the last few days. The deputy's murder was a big event for a small town like Bryson's Grove. He couldn't help but think there something more to it than just a random act of violence; the fact that the deputy's gun had never been found, the angle of the entrance wound, and the absence of blood splatter on the windshield. All these things had been discussed with the investigators and they all came up with the same idea. Roger Pinson had been shot somewhere else and was placed or driven to the scene in his patrol car. But where had he been for two hours, and what was he doing? And why had someone tried to make it look like a robbery or a retaliation of some sort?

Jake made notes of the location to be surveyed, filed the information he received in the proper location in his filing cabinet, and walked out the door. He would go home, get a good night's sleep, and take off in the morning. As he passed the boarding house, Charlotte was leaving, headed for the post office. He waved to her as he passed, and she sensed something strange. She just passed it off as repercussions from the last two day's events. She would call him later to see if he wanted some company, that is, if he didn't call her first. The phone rang in the sheriff's office, and it was Agent Miller from Knoxville.

"The print from the deputy's window produced a match in the FBI files." He said as the sheriff waited anxiously for the results. "I will be there tomorrow so we can continue the investigation."

"Anyone local?" the sheriff asked. "Yes, and we will need to get on with the investigation quick. Although I don't think there is much of a chance of this person leaving, we need to continue as fast as we can. I will be in your city tomorrow morning, and we can go from there." The agent calmly hung up the phone.

The sheriff sat there in wonder and disbelief,

"Never would have figured this," he thought.

The fingerprint on the deputy's patrol car belonged to Charles Davis, the manager of the paper mill. It seems that Mr. Davis had been arrested several years before on a DUI charge and that was the only offense he had ever committed, that is, up until this incident. He had some serious explaining to do.

Mr. Davis opened the door to his office and invited the two lawmen in.

"I am glad you are here," he said " I believe I have some more information on the young man you are looking for."

"Good" the agent replied, "and we have some more questions for you. We found your fingerprint on the passenger side window of Deputy Pinson's patrol car. How can you explain that?"

"That is impossible," Davis, replied, "I haven't been in a patrol car in years. The last and only time I have ever been arrested was for drinking and driving and that was five years ago. They reduced it to reckless driving and gave me probation for three years. I have been clean ever since."

"Regardless of what you say, your fingerprint was lifted at the scene, and verified through the FBI data base. You might want to call your lawyer and have him meet us at the sheriff's office in Bryson's Grove". Sheriff Thompson said.

"So what am I being charged with?" Mr. Davis asked.

"Suspicion of murder," agent Miller said.

"Although there is no formal charge being placed now, we have an extensive number of questions for you."

They placed Charles under arrest and read him his rights. As they handcuffed him and led him out to the car, he told his secretary to locate his assistant manager out in the plant and for him to take charge until he returned. They led him out to the patrol car and sat him in the back seat. As they pulled out into the highway headed back to Bryson's Grove, the officers thought they had the best clue of the case; or at least it would be a starting point.

When they got to the sheriff's office Mr. Davis called his longtime friend and attorney in Knoxville, Wilbur Starks. He explained the situation and Starks told him to sit tight until he could get there. It would be the next day before they could meet and talk in the sheriff's office, which meant Davis was spending the night in jail. Although it wasn't much, the fingerprint on the Deputy's patrol car window was enough to hold the suspect for further questioning. After securing the prisoner, they went into the sheriff's personal office to go over details of the case. Miller was particularly interested in the information sheriff Thompson had found out about the application of Byron Davis for the deputy position. The pieces to the puzzle were beginning to come together. The only thing to figure out now was a motive, but that would come they thought, just a matter of putting everything together.

By now the town was in a tailspin. The communication system had been put into place. It started out in the dry goods store, and had already graduated all the way to Annie's Café. Some of the townspeople knew Charles Davis. His wife had passed away several years ago from breast cancer and after that he kind of kept to himself. They had owned a small place out of town just west of the paper mill. Nothing to brag about, just a few acres and a horse barn. There wasn't much use in farming, so he just kept the place in hopes that his son would someday produce him some grandchildren, and they could come out and ride horses. By the time the story had reached Charlotte's place, it had been blown all out of proportion, as most gossip does. The rumors were from one end of the spectrum to the other. The stories ranged from drugs to the Taliban, depending on whom you got it from. Charlotte just listened to the story, mostly out of courtesy and passed it off after the old biddies left. Then she called Jake to check up on him and asked if he had heard the news. "No, but I am sure you are going to give me the 411." Jake said, "You usually wind up finding out what is going on before the newspaper does. By the way, wonder why there hasn't been anything in the local papers about this?" This was odd she thought; usually the paper had reports on everything, heck you couldn't stumble on the courthouse steps without someone noticing it and getting it to the paper.

The officers asked the local judge for a search warrant in order to search Davis' home and property; and after presenting the evidence, it was obtained. After securing the prisoner, they proceeded out to the Davis property and began to search the house. Not much was out of place. A few dirty dishes in the sink, some clothes in the laundry room, and coffee in the pot. They didn't really know what they were looking for, but any clue would be good. As they went through the drawers in his desk, one by one, there was nothing out of the ordinary. They found Davis' checkbook and it looked mostly normal. The usual weekly paychecks deposited to his personal account at the bank in Bryson's Grove were pretty consistent. The only thing that was out of sync was a large cash deposit that he had made just two weeks before. The amount was $50,000.00. This was almost the amount of salary the manager's position at the paper mill gave him on a yearly basis. "Wonder where this came from?" the agent said.

"We will just have to add that to the list of other questions we have for him." The sheriff said.

Room by room they searched, documented their findings and took pictures where it was necessary. There had been evidence of someone else staying there, but it wasn't known whom he or she was, or how long they had stayed. They left the house and tried to get into the garage. The door had a pad lock and a hasp on it. The agent went back to the trunk of his car and produced a set of bolt cutters.

"Just happened to have my pocket watch wrench with me," he said with a grin. "Never had any trouble gaining entry with this little fellow."

They cut the lock on the door and walked inside. There were the usual garage items, tools, ladders, petroleum products, etc. The garage was unusually clean. More so than the inside of the house. The only thing different was a stain on the floor just inside where the garage door closes. As they opened the door, they noticed that the stain was also on the outside of the building. After a careful examination, they determined that they needed the forensic experts out there to check out the house. The agent called his office in Knoxville and they notified him that they would be there in a couple of hours. "All we can do is wait, these guys are usually pretty punctual." He said.

> "I'll go down to the motel and get us a couple of cups of coffee," the sheriff said. "The motel isn't much, but the manager, Aaron Walker usually keeps a fresh pot of coffee all through the day."

"Sounds like a good idea to me," the agent replied, "I'll stay here and keep the locals out. There has been a lot of rubbernecking out on the highway, and I'll bet you a cup of coffee at Annie's that it won't be long until they start drifting out here to see what is going on."

With that the sheriff started down the highway to the Bryson Grove Motel. It was only about five miles away, and it wouldn't take too long to get there and back. The boring thing was going to be waiting on the forensic experts to get to the Davis home. They had to make sure the property was secure and that any possible evidence wouldn't be disturbed. The sheriff parked under the canopy and walked into the lobby of the motel. Sure enough, there sat Aaron with the newspaper and a fresh cup of coffee. You could smell the aroma as soon as you opened the door. Not to mention the stale cigarette smoke that lingered in the air also.

"How bout a couple cups of java?" The sheriff asked.

"Help yourself, ain't much going on and it don't look like the few customers I have are going to drink it." Aaron replied.

"Anything unusual been happening?" the sheriff asked.

"If you mean any strangers being around, the answer is no. Not much, other that the usual visitors. You know, the ones who sneak in here after a few beers from down the road, with someone else's wife or girlfriend. Not much changes here. Sorry to hear about deputy Pinson, didn't like him much, but nobody really did. Don't know what that young girl saw in him, but everyone deserves someone I guess."

"What young girl?" the sheriff asked. "He lived alone, and I didn't know that he was seeing anyone. He usually kept to himself."

"He spent the night here in the motel three days before you guys found him dead." Aaron replied,

" He had a pretty decent looking young girl with him and she left early the next morning. He brought her here in his patrol car and left her. A little while later, he came back in his pickup truck and spent the night. Just figured he had picked her up and brought her here for some companionship. They both left in his truck the next morning and that was pretty early."

"Did you get a look at her?" the sheriff asked.

"Not a very close up one, but I saw her as they got out of the patrol car and he let her into the room." Aaron told him.

"Would you be able to identify her from a picture?" The sheriff asked.

"Probably," Aaron answered, " she looked an awful lot like that young woman they found dead in the park the other day."

"What about your guest register?" the sheriff asked. Aaron laughed.

"You know that most people don't sign in, they just pay cash and spend a few hours. Most of them don't usually spend the whole night. They are just getting away from their husband's or wives long enough to get what they don't get at home."

The sheriff paid for the coffee and got into his patrol car. They had searched the deputy's house, and looked into the pickup truck parked in the garage, but they had not seen anything out of the ordinary. He would have the forensic guys check out Pinson's place also while they were here. His only living relative, an aunt in Nashville, had been contacted, but she wasn't due to arrive until this weekend. When the sheriff got back to the Davis residence, he told Miller about the conversation he had with Aaron. After discussing the possibilities, they called the motel and asked if anyone else had stayed in that room since Pinson had. Aaron said no, but the cleaning lady had cleaned the room. The sheriff advised Aaron to keep the room vacant and not to let anyone else in the room until they could get there. They would let the forensic team check the room also. Maybe there would be some sort of link. He would also have to contact the judge, fill him in on the events that just happened, and get a search warrant for Pinson's place too.

A couple of hours later they arrived. One of the team members had been on the scene at the park where the Sawyer girl's body had been found.

"Once you guys have finished here, I want you to process a room at the local motel, and also the Deputy's residence. There may or may not be a connection between the two deaths, but I want to find out if there is." The sheriff said to them as they started inside the house.

After a careful examination of the residence, there turned up no evidence of any wrongdoing. They found some evidence of someone other than the owner having slept in the spare bedroom as there were some hairs on the pillow and there had been a toothbrush left behind. They processed these items and came outside to the garage. The examiners checked the stains at the entrance to the garage doors and determined that it was blood. They took a sample of it from some grass that had grown up between the cracks in the concrete on the front of the garage floor, and looked around outside the building for any more clues. There had been two sets of tire tracks in the driveway. One was located in a direct line with the garage door as if it was used daily, and the other set had been found to the right of the drive, as if someone else had parked there for the night. The tire tracks were photographed and a plaster cast was made of the indentions in the earth. After the clues had been bagged and tagged, they proceeded to the motel. The sheriff had asked the forensic examiners if it would do any good to process the room, because it had already been cleaned.

"Just depends," the agent commented," if the cleaning lady wasn't too efficient, then we might find something. From what I remember about the motel from the day we checked the deputy's car, it doesn't look like the kind of place that gets a real good cleaning after someone uses one of the rooms. But we will see."

When they arrived at the motel, Aaron gave them the key and they entered the room. There was evidence that someone hade been there cleaning, as the bed sheets had been changed, and there was also evidence of a vacuum cleaner having been there. Two hours later, they had completely covered the room. There had been some traces of semen on the chair beside the bed, possibly some hair from one of the occupants between the bed and the nightstand, and there were fingerprints on the glasses that were left there. One of the glasses had been replaced and the other still had the plastic wrapping on it from not having been used. They found the cleaning lady and asked her how extensively she had cleaned the room. "I do what I normally do, I clean, change the linens, vacuum, and leave the matches and close the bible and put it in the drawer." She said.

"What do you mean, close the bible?" The examiner asked. "Most of the time when people read our bibles, the just leave them open and laying on the bedside table. That was the way I found it." She said. With that, the examiner took the Bible out of the drawer and examined the cover. The surface was smooth enough to have some fingerprints, and he processed it. He put the book in a plastic sleeve, and added it to the list of evidence they had found.

The last stop they made was the deputy's residence. The truck was parked in the garage just where Pinson had left it the last time he had driven it. They split up in order to get through sooner. Half of the four-team members processed the house and the other half processed the truck and the garage. They found some empty plastic cups from under the seat on both sides of the cab of the truck. Apparently the driver and the passenger had enjoyed some refreshments, what ever they were. They also photographed and made plaster casts of the tire tracks just outside of the garage. Jonathan thought the tracks looked a little too wide for an ordinary vehicle, and made a mental note to try and find out if there were any sport cars in the area that would take use high-speed tires. They processed these also and added them to the list of articles to examine.

The sheriff got a phone call from the jail. It seemed that the attorney for Mr. Davis had arrived and was highly agitated because no one was there to greet him.

"Tell him to have a seat, and we will be there shortly." He said.

"Damned attorneys are all just alike. They think they are the only people in the world that have something to do and they want it done on their schedule."

With that they locked up the deputy's garage and replaced the yellow caution tape around the driveway posts, to keep "visitors" out. The examiners bid them goodbye with promises of getting them the reports as soon as they were available. When the sheriff and agent Miller arrived at the jail, there sat the attorney, fuming. After a battle of words, they advised the attorney that the print on the deputy's patrol car belonged to Mr. Davis, and that they intended on holding him until further results from the evidence was obtained from the forensic examinations of Davis' home and garage; the room at the motel that the Deputy and an unknown young lady had spent the night; and the deputy's residence and garage and contents.

"I guess there isn't a bonding company in this one horse town, is it?"

The attorney snarled.

"Sorry," the sheriff replied, "there used to be, but he took his one horse and moved to Sevierville a few years ago. Not much money to be made here, but if he hears about this, he might just think it worth the while, and move back."

"Smartass," the attorney mumbled under his breath.

"I'll be back tomorrow with a court order having him out of jail!"

"Don't bet on it," the sheriff said "we are waiting on evidence from the forensic experts and we are going to keep him here until we get the results. Would you like to be here while we interrogate him?"

The Davis interview took quite a long time. At first he didn't want to say much. He just sat there and answered yes or no. When asked why his fingerprint was on the Deputy's window, he just said that he had been stopped for speeding and the deputy directed him to the patrol car so he could check his driving record. He was actually pretty stone faced most of the time, but when Agent Miller mentioned the blood samples that had been taken from the front of the garage, Charles Davis turned white as a sheet. He also told Davis that they had taken several articles of evidence from his home and garage and had sent them to the forensics laboratory in Knoxville for analysis.

"If there is anything you would like to tell us, now is the time to do it." Agent Miller said.

"It will be a lot easier on you if you fill us in on what happened, rather than us finding out the hard way."

Mr. Davis was asked about the $50,000.00 deposit he had made and his explanation was that his mother-in-law had a policy on his wife that he didn't know about; and they didn't find the policy until his mother-in-law had died a few months ago.

"I have the attorney and insurance companies names and contact numbers if you would like to check it out," he said." I have all of my important papers in a large plastic box under my bed. I know that isn't the safest place for them, but I am not much on banks or deposit boxes. I have records from the attorneys and the insurance company that will show where the money came from, if it is in fact any of your damned business!"

"That would be helpful on your part," Agent Miller said.

"It is kind of suspicious for you to deposit less than $1,000.00 per week in your checking account for more than a year, and then have a large sum of money show up all of a sudden. Not to mention the fact that we found your fingerprint on the window of a murdered officer's patrol car."

They had retrieved the large plastic box from under Charles' bed with what looked like a lot of important papers in it. They brought it in so he could produce the evidence of the origin of the money. He had kept pretty good records, as they took the top off the box, there were several manila envelopes inside and the one marked "settlement" provided a letter from the attorney and the insurance company with a copy of the check that he had received. "Well, that's' one," the sheriff thought;

"Now we have to get an explanation of where the blood came from." Charles Davis had no explanation for the blood. He swore that he didn't even know that it was there. As for the tire tracks, that could have been from his son's truck, his son's girlfriend's car, or from someone's vehicle that hunts on the Davis property. There had been several large deer bagged from this property in the last few years. Although he had a limited list of people who hunted on his property, he did let some of his friends hunt there.

His explanation made sense to the officers. They would just have to wait on the information from the forensic investigation. If necessary, they could contact all of the people who had used the property for hunting purposes and check their vehicles for a comparison to the evidence. It was just a waiting game until then. They had no actual evidence that Charles Davis was involved in the death of the Deputy, and at the advice of the judge, they released him into the custody of his attorney. He was instructed not to leave the county until the results of the investigation had been founded. The attorney and the suspect signed the affidavit and left the sheriff's office. They decided to stop for the day. It was around 6 p.m. and the agent already had his taste buds warmed up for some of Charlotte's apple pie. He left the sheriff in his office talking on the phone, and decided to stay over the night in town. They would go back out to the Davis property tomorrow and look around some more. All of the pieces to the puzzle were there he thought, it was just a matter of getting them in the right places.

Jake and Charlotte had just finished dinner, and were walking down the lane towards the old barn. The breeze was slightly blowing and the old oil lantern had a soothing glow to it. As they passed the old horse barn, she reached for his hand and squeezed it gently.

"What are you thinking about?" she asked.

"You seem a little out of sorts tonight."

"I can't really put my finger on it," he said.

"Too many things have happened in the last couple of weeks. Makes you think about a lot of stuff. If finding the girl wasn't enough, then I had to find Roger dead too. There is something awful strange about this whole situation. Somehow, I think all of this is related. I have lived here all of my life except for the time I was away in the Service, and I cannot remember the last time someone was murdered in this county."

"I know what you mean," she said.

"I moved back here because of all of the crime and stuff that was going on in the big city, and it makes me feel uneasy sometimes now that all of this has happened. Our peaceful and quiet little community has been victimized or something. Have things like this been going on around us and we have just been shutting our eyes to it, or have we just been ignoring it?" she asked with a puzzled look on her face.

"I can't explain it" Jake said. Most folks haven't been locking their doors in years, now you can almost feel the tension among them."

They had stopped by the fence and he was leaning against the corner post as if to say, "Kiss me." She stood on her tiptoes and gave him a soft kiss on the cheek. As he put his arms around her, he kissed her passionately and caressed her gently; she almost went limp.

"We need to get back to the house," he suggested. "We are about out of fuel for the lantern, and I don't want to be stumbling around here in the dark."

She knew that he was just making an excuse for not staying out there near the old horse barn. He knew that she had a fantasy of making love in the hay, and he wasn't in the mood to be pulling straw out of his underwear before going to bed tonight.

As they got closer to the house, he asked, "Are you staying the night?"

"Only if you want me to," she replied.

"I'll gather some firewood while you put your car in the garage." He said.

While he was gathering the firewood he thought about how nice it was to have her around. He had been thinking a lot about her lately, and he almost missed her when she was gone; hell, he missed her a lot. It was about time he settled down and quit roaming. He could arrange his working hours to be home just about every night, and they spent several nights a week together anyway. More and more of the townspeople were asking questions about them because they spent so much time together, and he wouldn't have her reputation scarred by him for love nor money. Besides, he had realized during the process of all of this drama going on that he had fallen in love with her, and he even thought about asking her to marry him. It had been quite a while since his divorce, and he wasn't getting any younger. He hadn't relished the thought of growing old by himself.

He stacked the wood in the wheelbarrow and started towards the house. She had already made it inside and was standing in the front window looking out at him as he made his way towards the house. She had the same warm feeling deep down inside as she usually did when she watched him work. Once she had been invited to go on an assignment with him. They had traveled two counties over to survey some land that had been annexed by the state for a new road. She had admired him standing beside the road looking through the instrument, wondering what he saw through the lens. Little did she know that as soon as she turned around to look the other way, he was looking at her. After finishing his assignment, they agreed to spend the night in the local motel and drive back the next day. The town was barely big enough to have a couple of fast food restaurants. Jake wondered why they wanted to build an interstate ramp there anyway. They got their food and retired to the room; but as fate would have it, they didn't get much to eat. She had been in the "mood" for a couple of weeks, and Jake had been so busy that he barely had time to get home from one assignment before going on to another one. She had already told herself that she was going to make love to him, whether he wanted to or not. That little trip turned into three of the most wonderful days in her life. They took the long way home the next day, and she really enjoyed the scenery. It was no secret to herself that she was in love with him, but she was really apprehensive about getting "attached" again. She had such a bad time with the first one she had made herself a promise that she wasn't going through that again. As he came through the door with the wood, she gently slapped him on the backside.

"You sure make a pair of jeans look good!" she said.

"And you need to keep your hands to yourself, young lady. I can be had, but I ain't no pushover." He jokingly remarked.

They both laughed aloud. He had been so busy with the wood that he hadn't noticed she had wrapped herself in his old wool blanket. As he put another log on the fire he turned around to ask if she wanted anything. About that time she dropped the blanket and stood there seductively,

"What did you have in mind?" she asked as she walked slowly toward him.

He didn't really know what to say, but he knew that he wanted her more than ever, and didn't want her to ever leave him. The fire burned slowly to glowing embers as they lay on the big sofa. Lucky for them the blanket was big enough to cover them both. Although they had let the fire burn down, they had warmth of their own between them, a fire that couldn't be put out. She fell asleep on the sofa, and he lay there watching her for a long time. He had made up his mind, he wanted her to be his wife, but he wasn't sure of how to go about talking her in to it. She had made mention that she didn't want to be married again. He thought a lot about what she had said; all he had to do now was to convince her that she needed to change her mind. As he slowly drifted off to sleep, she had a soft smile on her face. She was right where she wanted to be.

She awoke the next morning to the smell of fresh coffee. Sometime during the night he had picked her up and carried her to the bedroom. As she sat upright in the bed, he entered the room with two steaming cups of coffee.

"Good morning my love," he said.

This startled Charlotte, as he had never mentioned that word except in casual sentences.

He handed her the coffee and kissed her gently on the lips.

"I have something to say, and I hope it comes out right," he stammered.

"I love you," he said, " and I cherish every minute we are together. The quiet evenings, the long walks, and the soft hugs and kisses make my life complete. The more I am with you, the more I want to be. I have been trying to muster up the courage to tell you, but until now, I haven't been able to get the words out. I don't want to scare you off, but I had to tell you how I feel."

She didn't know what to say. Here she was with the most wonderful man she had ever known, and knew she was in love with him, but she was surprised that he would say these things. He never ceased to amaze her.

"Somewhere behind that 12 foot wall I knew there was a soft spot," she replied "but I didn't know just how soft it was. You are a wonderful man, Jake Stuart, and every time I get near you, my heart wants to jump out of my chest. I never knew that anyone could make me feel the way you do. I love you, too. I have wanted to tell you that for a long time, but was afraid that if I did you might just retreat further back behind that wall."

"OK, so where do we go from here?" he asked.

"No where in particular," she said.

"Nothing should change just because we both admitted to each other that we are in love. As a matter of fact, it should make us closer. I love you more every day. Each time we are in each other's arms, I feel closer to you. There is a warm calm feeling that spreads over me whenever I am with you; a feeling of safety and well-being."

"I know," he said "I really look forward to each time we are together, and when you leave, it seems like a small part of me is gone. When I am away on assignment, I am always thinking of how long it will take to bring me back to you."

He sat the coffee cup on the bedside table and as he looked into her beautiful green eyes, she let the sheet fall and drew him closer to her. They rolled over in the bed and as she lay there looking down into his eyes she knew she was in the right place; and hoped that she could stay there forever.

"Looks like I am going to be late for work," he softly said, almost in a whisper.

" That's ok," she said, "I know the owner and I will put in a good word for you. I doubt that you have too much to worry about."

"In that case I'll take a little longer this morning," he said, "there isn't any place that I had rather be than right here."

With that she kissed him softly on the lips for a long time. His gentle touch sent electric sensations up her spine and echoed through the depths of her soul. As their passions reached their peak, she whispered in his ear what she had wanted to shout to the world."

He smiled and gave her a gentle hug. "It is going to be a good day," he thought. It wasn't as hard as he thought it was going to be, although he wasn't expecting the response she gave him. He had thought she liked him a lot, but was afraid that her previous marriage had ruined his chances of having her all for himself.

"Now all I have to do is to figure out how to keep her!" he thought.

Sue Ellen was about to put what was left of the pies and cakes in the refrigerator as Agent Miller walked through the door.

"Got anything left for supper?" he asked.

"Not much," she replied. "Just enough to fill a hungry man's stomach."

"Then that's what I'll have." Was his reply.

Sue Ellen always had a soft spot for a man in a uniform. She had dated someone who had been in the army, and every time she got those old pictures out, she got chills. This was the third time the agent had been in Annie's and he seemed friendlier every time. She was about twenty minutes from closing, and she wasn't in much of a mood to be kept late. She had plans for the evening, and didn't want them to change. She and her girlfriends had made plans for a night on the town, such as it was, and she was looking forward to it. It had been a while since she had been intimate with anyone, and she was feeling the urge. She sat the last of the glasses into the dishwasher and as she emerged from the kitchen she noticed a smile on the agent's face. Apparently he had been watching her work, and she hadn't noticed.

"In a hurry to leave?" He asked as she scurried around.

"Have a hot date?"

"Not really," she replied.

"Just me and the girls are going out on the town tonight and I need to hurry home and get ready."

"Can you recommend someplace to get a drink in this town?" he asked.

"The only place around here is the local tavern, but I didn't think you guys frequented places like that." She told him with a grin.

"Just because I am a law enforcement officer, doesn't mean that I am not human. I enjoy the same things everyone else does, I just have to be a little more discreet about what I do and how I do it."

Sue Ellen sat down at the table with Agent Miller; "I am sorry," she said. "I wasn't meaning to be rude, I guess I was in a hurry and wasn't paying attention to you. My name is Sue Ellen, and yours?"

"Jonathan Miller pleased to meet you."

"There isn't much left from dinner," she said.

"I can whip you up something from the grill if they haven't already cleaned it. The grouchy old cook usually tries to stop cooking about half an hour before we close so he won't have to wait around after closing to get things cleaned up and ready for the morning rush."

"That won't be necessary," Miller said

"How about a piece of that chocolate pie and a cup of coffee?"

"Coming right up " she replied and headed off to the cooler to retrieve the next to the last piece. One of the things the cook was noted for was the fact that she could make a mean chocolate pie. When she returned, she decided to call her friends and tell them that she would catch up with them later, that she had a late customer come in and needed to stay.

They sat and talked for a couple of hours. She found out that Agent Miller had been married and his wife had died after a boating accident. He had been single for three years and hadn't been in a serious relationship since. She told him of her tumultuous past with her abusive husband. After she started talking to Jonathan, she was really surprised at herself. She had never talked to a stranger like that before. There was something uncannily smooth about the feeling she had talking to him, and it didn't seem hard at all to talk to him about anything. The conversation continued as they walked out the door. He had stayed while she closed the place up, and walked her out to her car. As she opened the door and threw in her apron and her purse, she turned around and thanked him for staying with her. As he looked into her eyes he could see she was excited and maybe even a little bit nervous. Little did he know just how nervous she was. He bent over and kissed her gently on the lips. She responded with a hug and kissed him in return.

He pulled himself away and told her to be careful and have a good time.

"Can I have your number?" he asked.

She thought for a moment, and almost declined. But she thought that if he wanted to he could get it from her driver's license or whatever methods they use to get whatever information they need. Besides, she kind of liked the way he kissed her and he was a right handsome guy, so what the heck.

"Sure, here is my cell phone number. I am not home most of the time, and that would be a better number than any." She nervously told him.

He handed her one of his business cards and told her that she could reach him most anytime after 9 am and most any evenings. He kissed her again and bade her goodnight. As he turned around and walked away, she noticed how well he filled out a pair of slacks. She almost wanted to call the girls and tell them that she had changed her mind and go grab a handful of the agent's ass, but nixed the idea for a better time and place. As he walked into the front door of the bed and breakfast, the butterflies finally left his stomach. "Hmmm, guess I haven't for gotten how to kiss a woman anyway." He almost felt sad again, but decided that it was about time that he started going out again. As he walked up the stairs, he didn't notice Charlotte in the living room. She had driven by the parking lot of the restaurant just as the agent had kissed Sue Ellen. Deep down inside she was happy for her. She was a good woman and deserved someone nice in her life; she had enjoyed her share of bastards in the world. Maybe it was her time to be blessed.

Breakfast was always an interesting time of the day in Bryson's Grove. Especially at Charlottes. The biscuits were soft and flaky, and the homemade sausage gravy was a delicacy rivaled only by the egg casserole that she made on occasion. She thought the agent might enjoy it and she hadn't made it in a while so there it was. There were three other couples staying there. They had made plans to drive out into the country and look at the leaves, the biggest drawing card up until now. This time of the year in east Tennessee, you had better to have made preparations a long time ago because if you hadn't, there weren't many places that you could find a room. Charlotte had built up quite a clientele. Most of the patrons were repeats from the year past, and once you stay there and sample the hospitality, most everyone wants to come back. After breakfast, Jonathan walked over to the sheriff's office. Sheriff Thompson had been there long enough to make a pot of coffee and he offered the agent a cup.

"No thanks," he said. "I just finished breakfast at the boarding house and couldn't handle anything else."

"If you did that you won't be worth a damn for the rest of the morning. That woman doesn't know the meaning of no and she whips up one hell of an egg casserole. If you ate there, you should be about ready for a nap." He said

"Yep, she sure does, any word from Knoxville?" he asked.

"There was a phone call earlier, but not much information." He said.

"Some of the tire tracks were from a vehicle that uses high speed tires. The tread design and the width of the tires aren't from an average vehicle. They were from the ones that we cast at the Davis place. Let's go back out there and see what we can come up with."

Agent miller agreed and walked out to the car. As he was getting in, he noticed Sue Ellen walking across the street. She smiled and walked over to the car.

"Good morning," he said as she approached the vehicle. "How was the hen party?"

She laughed aloud and told him that they just sat around and bashed all of the men they knew.

"I'll bet your ears were burning," she said.

"Why, Sue Ellen, I am surprised that you are the type of woman who would kiss and tell."

"I didn't tell them anything, I just let them think what they wanted to!" she replied.

About that time the sheriff came out and got into

the car. Sue Ellen excused herself and as she was walking away, the agent said " see you later."

"I hope so!" was her reply and sheepishly grinned as she turned around.

"Anything I need to know about the girl?" he asked the sheriff.

"Not really Jonathan" the sheriff said, "she has been single for quite a while and doesn't date much as far as I know. She apparently came from an abusive relationship and has been divorced for some time. Her husband was sent to prison for something I know nothing about and she moved here several years ago to get a fresh start. She has always had a good personality about her and most all of the people in town like her. Never heard anyone say anything bad about her."

"I stopped by the restaurant last night, and we had quite a good time talking. She seems like a fun person, and I like redheads." Jonathan said.

Driving out of town, Jonathan thought how Bryson's Grove seemed like a nice town. He had lived in a bigger city for quite some time now and with all of the friendly people around here, it may not be a bad place to come and stay for a while. Depending on how long it took him to finish his investigation, he would enjoy his visit here. As they passed the bank, the agent noticed the new Lexus parked out front.

"Who owns that?" he asked.

"It belongs to the banker's wife." The sheriff said. "Nice little piece of machinery isn't it?"

"You don't see those kind of vehicles in small towns

like this. Most of the luxury cars are Cadillac's, BMW's, or Lincolns. " The agent said.

"Yea, and most small towns don't have a banker that is married to a woman 25 years younger than he is that has a New York taste for everything," the sheriff replied.

"Let's take a look at the tires on her car when we get back," the agent said.

"I'm not that familiar with the tread pattern on high performance tires, but I'll bet you a cup of coffee that that little honey of a vehicle has some pretty expensive paws on it."

"OK," the sheriff said, "we'll look at them when we get back. I have wanted to get a closer look at the vehicle anyway. Never been close to a car that cost $80,000.00. I am kind of curious as to what it has in it." The clouds were giving away to some sunshine as they drove toward the main highway. As they passed the motel, Jonathan's thoughts drifted back to Sue Ellen. He would call later and see if she would be available tonight. Maybe they could get together and get to know each other a little better.

There was still quite a bit of dew on the grass as they got out of the car in Charles Davis' driveway. As they walked around the side of the garage, they noticed that there was a pickup truck parked behind it. After a close inspection of the vehicle, there was evidence that it had been there for a while. The hood was cool and the windows were still wet from the condensation. They hadn't much more that got around the end of the truck when a hunter came out of the woods. They startled each other and as the hunter approached them, the sheriff asked who he was.

"I work for Mr. Davis at the paper mill. He lets me hunt here sometimes. I have bagged a couple of big bucks off of his farm and I always give him some venison when I process the deer."

"What do you know about Mr. Davis?" the agent asked.

"Not much, he keeps to himself pretty much. I have talked to him in the cafeteria at the paper mill several times. That is how I found out that he lets a few people hunt on his property." The young man said.

"Anyone else from the mill hunt here?" the sheriff asked.

"Not that I know of," the young man replied. "Mr. Davis told me that he doesn't let just anyone on his property and if I wanted to continue hunting out here, that I shouldn't tell anyone else about it."

"OK," the sheriff replied. "Thanks for the information. We are conducting an investigation into the death of a local officer and this place is off limits until we finish the investigation. I need your name and drivers license number in case we need to talk to you further. It would be a good idea if you didn't come back out her for a while." With that the young man gave the sheriff the information he requested, got into his truck and left. Jonathan wrote down the young man's license number and made a mental note to check it out against the information he provided when he got back to town. They scanned the area around the garage and even walked out into the woods for a short distance but found nothing out of the ordinary. When they got back to the rear of the garage, Jonathan took pictures of the tire tracks where the truck had been parked. After a short conversation about Mr. Davis, they got back into the patrol car and started towards town. When they got back to town, the Lexus was gone.

"Must have had some serious shopping to do," the sheriff commented. "She doesn't usually come into town unless she needs to get some money."

" Must be a tough life," Jonathan said, "guess someone has to do it."

They went into the sheriffs office to check for information from the Forensics guys in Knoxville, and after a short phone call, there was not anything new available.

"How about some lunch? Been a long time since coffee and rolls this morning." The sheriff asked.

"Sure," Jonathan agreed. He was getting hungry, and besides, it would give him a chance to talk to Sue Ellen again. As they walked across the street to the restaurant, she could see them coming. She hurriedly went to the employee's restroom and took her perfume out of her bag. She had hoped the agent would come by today and had it ready just in case. It had been a busy day, and she didn't want him to suspect her nervousness. As he and the sheriff sat down at one of the tables by the window, she snagged two menus and started toward them. As she approached the table, his smile seemed to get larger by the step. He was almost embarrassed. It had been a long time since he had been giddy about a woman and it almost reminded him of his high school days. She left the menus and retreated for orders of tea and coffee. When she returned they had opted for the special. A generous helping of roast beef on open-faced sandwiches with mashed potatoes and gravy. She hustled back to the kitchen to turn in the order. One of the servers had called in sick for the day and it left them shorthanded. She was especially aggravated because she knew if he did come in for lunch, that she would probably be too busy to talk to him. They exchanged smiles and it wasn't long until they had finished their lunch. He had wanted to ask her out for tonight, but didn't get the chance. He offered to pay the lunch ticket and the sheriff didn't argue with him. When he walked to the register to pay Sue Ellen had just finished checking out another customer. "What time are you through today?" he asked.

"I should be through by 5:00 or so." She replied.

"Would you care to go to a movie or something tonight? Sorry about asking you so late, but we were anticipating some information on the case and I figured that we would be working late. Unfortunately, there wasn't anything new on the case. If it is an inconvenient time, we can make it later."

"I'll be ready at 7 she said. Here is my address." She said. She had written her address on the back of the receipt from the cash register. He smiled, pocketed the receipt, and turned and walked out the door.

For a minute, her heart raced; but not as much as it would tonight she thought.

The sheriff retired to his office and the agent got in his car and drove toward Charlotte's bed and breakfast. He had forgotten that he needed to check out because of prior registrations and when he walked in the door, she reminded him that someone was supposed to be checking into his room that evening. "Damn'" he thought, "that's right. I completely forgot. I'll only be a few minutes getting my things together."

He told Charlotte as he hurried up the stairs. When he returned a few minutes later, he paid his obligations with a state voucher.

"Got any suggestions about where I can find a place for the night? He asked.

"Not really, unless there is room at the motel on the outskirts of town. I thought you only needed the room for one night."

"Me too," he said.

"Something else came up today and I need to stay over again."

As he was walking out the door, she said to him

"If they don't have any vacancies, let me know and I will see what I can find for you. This time of the year is pretty busy for everyone, but you never know, my reservations for the night might cancel. They have until 6 p.m. to arrive. If they don't I'll hold it for you."

"Thank you," he replied and walked out the door to his car. As he drove out of town, he passed the motel and remembered the condition of the rooms when they looked them over.

"I'll take my chances on the cancellations," he thought.

"If it don't work out, I'll just take a shower at the jail, and sleep there."

The afternoon seemed to drag on. After the lunch rush not many people came into the restaurant and this left Sue Ellen with plenty of time to think about what she should wear on her "first date" with Jonathan. He had driven to Deputy Pinson's house to check the scene to make sure nothing had been tampered with.

At precisely 6:55 Jonathan walked up and knocked on Sue Ellen's door. The small house had a clean and tidy look to it. She was ready but invited him in and told him she would be a few minutes. She couldn't let him know that she had been ready for 30 minutes and that she had changed clothes 5 times.

About ten minutes later she re appeared and they decided to leave.

"Do you mind driving?" He asked. "I am not allowed to transport anyone in my car unless it is on police business."

"Not at all," she replied. "Where to?"

"Where is the nearest movie theatre?" he asked.

"Not too close, we have about a 40 minute drive. How about we get some dinner and then come back here and watch one on the tube. I rented a couple yesterday and haven't had chance to watch them."

"Sounds good to me," he said.

The drive to the restaurant was short and comfortable. The conversation was light and almost nervous. Jonathan hadn't been on a real date for quite some time. He had a female friend that worked with him, but there wasn't anything romantic about their trips to the movies or dinners. She had been divorced for quite a while and just wanted a man around to pal around with. That was fine with him, he hadn't really given most women a second look, that is until the first time he had seen Sue Ellen cross the street in front of the sheriff's office.

"Anything new on the deputy" she asked.

"Not really, but I couldn't tell even if there was." He replied.

"He was a strange kind of guy." She said,

" I went to the movies with him once and we went to dinner also, but he never really seemed like the dating type. He was always talking about his job and how he liked to chase people down that were speeding and write them a ticket. He called a couple of more times, but I told him that I just wasn't interested."

"How did that make him feel?" Jonathan asked.

"Don't really know, he didn't have much to say for a couple of weeks and then all of a sudden he came into the restaurant one day and just acted like there was never anything wrong. I was apprehensive at first, but after a couple of days, I just shrugged it off and let it go. We had been pretty good friends ever since."

Jonathan really didn't want to discuss the case, but

the conversation had pretty much gone south anyway, so it was something to keep it alive.

The dinner was pretty good. Most of the little country restaurants that had popped up around the paper mill served pretty good food. It was a treat to get out of Bryson's Grove and visit another eating-place instead of the one where she worked. One conversation led to another, and after a while he felt almost comfortable with her. On the drive back to her house, they even managed a joke or two to liven things up.

She opened the door and invited him in. As they sat on the sofa in the living room, the conversation slowly drifted towards him and his past; something he wasn't very comfortable with. After a couple of short answers, she suggested the movie and she quickly agreed. As they settled down for the evening, the wind slowly tossed the chimes on the back porch and rustled the leaves in the trees. "Won't be long till we will need the fireplace," she said.

"Yes I know, " he replied. "I hate cold weather, kind of wish sometimes I could move south for the winter."

She sat beside him again, and for a few minutes there seemed like nothing to say. All at once the movie started, and he was grateful for the beginning. For the next two hours there was only small talk, and when the movie was over he thanked her for the hospitality. As he was walking out the door, he turned and softly kissed her on the cheek. Nervously, she gave him a hug and thanked him for a wonderful time. As he turned to walk away she squeezed his hand and he turned and gave her a long passionate kiss. Her heart seemed to melt away. It had been so long since she felt this way, and she didn't want to let him go. He knew that it wasn't the appropriate time, so he just simply asked if they could see each other again. "I certainly hope so, " she said. With that he slowly walked down the walkway to his vehicle.

As he drove away, he almost felt like a schoolboy leaving the cheerleader's house after their first date.

"This little town isn't too bad after all," he thought. "Might not be a bad place to live."

When he drove past the bed and breakfast, he noticed the vacancy sign in the window. Charlotte had told him that if the reservations hadn't shown up or had cancelled that the sign would be in the window. He walked inside and the key to his room was in the box on the counter. As he slowly walked up the stairs he thought of the sparkle in those green eyes; yes he would see her again. He had some time off and if she could swing it, he would take her on a tour of the mountains for a couple of days. He made the trip on his Harley last year about this time, and the scenery was absolutely beautiful. He would almost be his next paycheck that she would like the ride.

The report from the forensics lab in Knoxville was in the sheriff's office the next morning. The tire tracks that were in the driveway next to Roger Pinson's truck were high performance 50 series and the tread pattern was specially made for the Lexus SC convertible. One of those sporty "little fellers" as the barbershop patrons would call it every time Diana Turner would park hers in front of the bank. There was a cut about 3 inches long running across the tread from the castings. Also there were fingerprint identifications from the plastic drink cups hidden under the passenger side of the deputy's truck. The fingerprints were matched to Diana Sawyer Turner, the last known address being from an affluent neighborhood in upper New York State.

Just as Jonathan was walking into the sheriff's office, the phone rang. The investigator had run the blood samples from in front of the garage, and they indeed matched Roger Pinson's.

"Interesting little story," the sheriff said. "Looks like we need to talk to the banker's wife."

"Know where to find her?" Jonathan asked.

"Well; we can start out at the house and if she isn't there, we can just wait for the credit cards to run out and talk to her when she gets home. When she gets bored, she visits her only close relative, which is a sister in a little town just south of Nashville.

The sheriff replied. "Maybe we should start out at the bank and see what Andrew has to say about this." A quick phone call to the bank revealed that the banker had a board of directors meeting to attend in Knoxville today and he probably wouldn't be back until later on in the evening or tomorrow morning.

"Oh well, we'll just ride out to the ranch and see what we can conjure up." The sheriff suggested. Jonathan wondered why the sheriff referred to it as the "ranch" that is until they started down the driveway.

About ½ mile off the roadway they parked in front of the garage. The sound of the river gravel crunching under their boots alarmed the dogs and they started barking loudly. They walked up to the front door and rang the doorbell. Isabella, the maid and housekeeper answered the door on the second ring.

"Morning sheriff," she said as she opened the door.

"Morning," he replied. "Is Mrs. Turner home?"

"No sir, she didn't come home last night. Mr. Andrew left for the city last night and shortly after he left, Mrs. Diana left too. She had a bag packed and said that she was going to see her sister in Nashville and stay a couple of days while Mr. Andrew was gone."

"Did she drive her car?" Jonathan asked.

"Yes she did, she said that she was going to drive it to the airport and fly to Nashville. I couldn't understand why she would do that, looks to me like that would be going the other way. She and Mr. Andrew had a few words before he left. She told him that she wanted a new car, and he told her no that the one she had was less than a year old, and that she would have to keep it until he decided she could have another one." Isabella said.

"Do you have her sister's address by any chance?" The sheriff asked.

"No, I don't", Isabella replied, "but I have her phone number in case of an emergency." The two officers took down the phone number and left. As they were driving away, the sheriff looked over at Jonathan and said, " Are you thinking what I am thinking?"

"Don't know," Jonathan said, "but I'll bet we need

to find that car before she has a chance to do something with it."

A quick call to the local highway patrol office yielded the information needed on Diana's sister. The phone number that she left was listed to a Theresa Gail Morgan Route 3 Allisonia, TN. The next phone call they made was to the Williamson County sheriffs department. After a short talk with the deputy in charge, they agreed to drive by the residence and see if the car was there.

"Looks like we need to go see the judge and get a warrant. This might get a little sticky. Especially if we find that cut on the tire. At this point she is just needed for questioning, but you can never tell." The sheriff said.

Bradley Manning had just finished writing his daily quota of tickets for the speed trap in Eagleville when he got the call on the radio. The dispatcher told him to drive by the Morgan residence on Horton Highway and advise if a white Lexus with Tennessee license WLKPT was in the driveway. The officer acknowledged the request and started through the country road that connects the two southern middle Tennessee towns. Nothing much happens out here in the country, unless someone runs off the road, most of the deputies answer fire calls and traffic accidents. Nothing has really happened since old man Morgan, Theresa's grandfather shot at the sheriff when they came to destroy his moonshine still. Or at least that was the way the story goes. Most of the residents in Williamson County moved there because the schools were better and the taxes were lower. In the last few years it had become a safe haven for some of the country music stars and other effluents that just wanted to get away from the hustle and bustle of Music City, but still be able to commute in a reasonable amount of time. The only problem was that most of the property had been inflated so much in the last few years, that if you wrote a ticket to an every day person they would bitch and moan because they couldn't buy groceries for paying the ticket. The deputy's usual answer was that they needed to move back to where they could afford to live.

As he passed the Methodist Church, the mayor of College Grove waved at the officer as he passed. He was very efficient at listening to the police scanner and trying to be around when the deputies would make calls in or near his city. He wasn't really the mayor, but everyone called him that. When the deputy passed the residence, sure enough, there sat the Lexus. As he drove past the house, he radioed the dispatcher and asked if there were any wants or warrants on the person in the car. The dispatcher replied to the negative, and to drive by a couple of times during his shift to keep surveillance on the vehicle.

In the meantime, sheriff Thompson and Jonathan Miller had rousted the judge and told him of the fingerprints and the information on the vehicle's tires. The judge agreed to give them a warrant so they could at least question her about the fingerprints and check the comparison of the vehicle's tires. After notifying the deputy that the driver of the Lexus was wanted for questioning, he parked across the street in the parking lot of the store and waited. After a copy of the warrant was faxed to the sheriffs' office in Williamson County, a detective met the deputy at the house and they knocked on the door. Theresa came to the door with a glass of wine in one hand and a cigarette in the other.

"Can I help you gentlemen?" she asked.

"We are looking for Ms Diana Turner, mam. Is she here?"

"No, she went shopping with my daughter and probably won't be back until after midnight." Was her reply.

"No where around here am I familiar with a place that stays open after 10:00 p.m." the detective said.

"I'll be happy to tell her to call you when she returns, however I do not know when that will be. The last time she visited here, she was gone for three days. When her husband goes out of town on these trips, she stays gone as long as she can." Teresa said.

"Thanks, we will check back tomorrow morning. Here is one of my business cards, and please tell her to call me when she returns. It is very important." With that the officers stepped off the porch and walked towards their cars. As they passed the Lexus, the detective placed his hand on the hood and it was still warm. "She hasn't been here very long," he said. "Bet you half of next week's salary she is somewhere around here."

"We can always go back and search the house. If she is there, she will turn up somewhere." The deputy said.

"Naw, let's just watch the place," he said, " Maybe

she will get antsy and make a mistake. I am not sure what is going on, I am going to call the TBI officer and get the lowdown on what is going on with this case."

They both drove away from the house. There were only two directions that she could get out of town and they could stop just outside of the city limits and see almost all the way down the main highway just in case she tried to leave. After a thirty-minute conversation with Jonathan, the detective agreed to watch the highway for a while just to see if she would appear. Sure enough, about two hours after they had been to the house, the Lexus came slowly down the highway. The officer let her pass and pulled in behind her. He ran the license number just to be sure, and sure enough, it was listed to Diana Turner of Bryson Grove Tennessee. He turned on his emergency lights, and she started to speed up.

"Dammit," he said "looks like she is going to run!"

He sped up and picked up the microphone for the police radio. The deputy had seen the car pull out from his hiding point, and joined in the chase. By the time they reached the forks of 31A and 41A they were doing well over 100 mph. They had requested another car to try to intercept her at the next intersection, but as the additional officer got to the intersection, she had just passed. On the radio the detective had told the dispatcher that the car was traveling in excess of 110 mph. A roadblock was set up at the four way stop at highway 96 and Horton Highway. There were four police cruisers and one highway patrol officer. As she approached the intersection of state highway 840 and

Horton Highway, she could see the reflections of the blue emergency lights up ahead. By this time she had slowed up enough to slam on the brakes, power slide the car, and turn left onto the ramp headed west. The detective was close enough on her that he almost hit her as she slid into the turn. On the ramp she accelerated again and they were off to the races. She had never been very far on this stretch of the highway, but she had seen it on the map and thought if she could get far enough ahead of them, maybe she could get off on a side road and hide for a while until she could call someone to come and get her. She had had an affair with one of the local real estate brokers in the area, and surely she could call him for help. Hell, she helped him hide some gravestones on a piece of property that he had sold; surely he would help her get to the airport or something.

She could see the reflection of the police lights in the distance behind her and thought that if she didn't do something quick, they would be catching up to her. Those damned plastic cups in Roger's truck. She thought about that several times. She had wiped the doors clean of the blood and fingerprints after the shooting, and thought she had removed all of the evidence. She never knew what Andrew did with Roger's gun, but she was sure glad he didn't use it on her too. She had drunk too much that night and was almost out of it when they were caught. Roger and his damned crazy ideas. They could have been at the motel having the usual good time that they were accustomed to, but no, he had wanted to go somewhere different.

She looked down at the speedometer and it was pegged at 150 mph. As she looked up she saw the sign stating that the roadway ended in 500 feet. She geared down the transmission and as she hit the brakes, the tires skidded in the loose gravel; the last thing she would remember would be the rock wall in the apex of the curve of the ramp onto Interstate 65. The car slid sideways into it. As she drew her last breath, she thought of the look on Andrew's face just before he pulled the trigger.

As the chase cars came upon the accident, they knew there was no hope for the driver. Too many times they had seen this happen. They immediately called for life flight, but as they got to the vehicle, they could see her crumpled body twisted inside the car. They had called for the extrication unit because the car was damaged so badly they couldn't get the door open. As the fire department got there, they cut the top off and the dashboard away from her. A paramedic had already pronounced her dead at the scene, but they still rushed her to the hospital. The car was impounded and under the request of Jonathan Miller and Sheriff Thompson, they didn't want anyone fooling around with any of the contents. It took the better part of an hour to get the accident scene cleaned up. After the identification officers took the pictures, and the highway patrol officers finished the report, they put the car on a flatbed wrecker and hauled it to the impound yard. There had been nothing inside the car, nothing in the glove box, the console, or even in the door panels.

Usually you will find some personal articles in the vehicle the trooper stated later to Jonathan, but this one was relatively clean. They couldn't get the trunk open because of the impact, but they left that chore to the investigating officers on the way there. By the time Jonathan and the sheriff got there the vehicle had been moved to the wrecker yard and locked behind a fence. They had it transferred to the local TBI headquarters in Nashville, a few miles away because it was suspect in a murder investigation of a police officer. A thorough examination of the tires revealed the tread pattern was the same as the tracks found beside Roger Pinson's pick up truck. The left front tire had a 3-inch cut across the tread pattern that matched the one in the casting. Diana's sister Teresa had been called to identify the body. When she arrived at the hospital she was carrying a small journal with her. When she was questioned by Jonathan Miller about the reason for her sister's sudden visit, she gave the book to the investigator and told him to read it. Diana told her just before she left the house that night, "If anything happens to me, give this to the police." Theresa had told the officers that Diana had told her that her husband Andrew was going to a board meeting and that when he returned, they were going to settle up on some things that needed to be cleaned up. "She was afraid for her safety," Theresa said.

"She has told me more than once that she was afraid that the developers that were trying to get old man Bryson's land were crooked and that if Andrew kept asking them for more money and didn't produce the land, that he would be in real trouble."

"Did your sister ever mention Roger Pinson?" Jonathan asked.

"Is that the local deputy sheriff in Bryson Grove?" she asked

"Why do you ask?" he said.

"Diana told me that she was having an affair with a local deputy sheriff. She said he was a speed freak, loved to drive her car fast, but wrote the hell out of tickets for people speeding themselves. She said that they met one night after she had been drinking and he stopped her for speeding. One thing led to another and after he had called her a couple of times, she decided to go out with him. Her husband wasn't taking care of her and she needed someone who could. The met at a little bar outside of town and usually wound up at the deputy's house. She wouldn't go anywhere in public with him, other than one trip to a local motel when someone was staying at Roger's house. She figured that she would be safe at his house because it was so far off the road that you had to drive up damned near to the house before you could see anything."

"Have you read anything in the journal?" Jonathan asked.

"No, but I probably should have. If I had, maybe she would still be alive right now. She was afraid her husband was going to kill her. That was the reason she was here. She was scared to death when she left, I begged her to stay and talk to the officers, but she said she had to get out of town quick."

Jonathan asked the clerk in at the police station to take the woman's statement and after doing so she could leave. As she walked out of the police station she turned to him and gave him a puzzled look. Almost as if she wanted to say something else, but was afraid to.

Jonathan took the journal and put it into his briefcase. He would read the contents when he got back to Bryson Grove. Right now he had to finish up the investigation and get this part of it closed out. He had thought about calling Sue Ellen, but he knew that wouldn't work, because she would be full of questions about what was going on and he couldn't tell her. He wanted to hold her, kiss her and make love to her.

They finished up the investigation and made arrangements for the car to be transported to the TBI office in Sevierville. The sun was just coming up and they knew that they would be endangering themselves and others if they tried to drive back without some rest. He pulled into the parking lot of the Marriott off interstate 65 south and he and the sheriff registered for two rooms for the night. Many things were going through his mind, but one thing was for sure, he was finally going to get to the bottom of the murder of Roger Pinson, and he was almost sure that Diana's husband had something to do with it.

As he took a shower and ordered room service of coffee and rolls, he picked up the journal and opened the cover to the front page. To whom it may concern, was the first sentence. That was as far as he got. The coffee and rolls were delivered and although they were there, he fell asleep before he got a chance to enjoy them. He slept for about 4 or 5 hours and would have slept longer, but the phone rang waking him up. The manager had transferred a call to him from the sheriff's room. It was Sue Ellen. She had gotten a phone call from her ex-husband. He had been in the penitentiary for the last five years for spousal abuse and said that he had gotten out and wanted to come and visit her. She was afraid to see him, and wanted some advise from Jonathan as to what she needed to do. She had tried Jonathan's cell phone number and couldn't get through. She knew the sheriff was with him, and as a last ditch effort called the sheriff's number trying to reach him. By the time Jonathan got to her on the phone, she was in tears and almost hysterical. Her ex husband had told her that he would kill her if she were still around when he got out of jail. Jonathan made a couple of phone calls and found out that Sue Ellen's ex had not been let out of jail, and that he had made the phone call from inside just to harass her. He called the local authorities at the prison, and a hearing was to be set to charge him. He was forbidden from ever talking to Sue Ellen again, and if he got within one mile of her, he would immediately go back to jail.

Jonathan called Sue Ellen back and told her that her ex was still in jail, and there was no threat to her. He told her that he would be back the next day and they should try to get together.

With that he decided that he couldn't go back to sleep. He was interested in the contents of the journal, and decided to take a shower and get to work on reading it.

The first entry was more than four years old. She and Andrew had been married only for a year when he had his first heart attack. The blood pressure medicine and the

Blood thinner had contributed to his already limited sexual performances. She had to go outside the marriage to find satisfaction. Andrew suspected as much, but he never said much about it. He was just happy to have her with him. He roamed in many effluent circles and she was good arm candy when they needed to be seen in public. And she really knew how to play the part. Whenever they were at a function, she expected everyone to notice her when she entered the room. He was the envy of many a young man.

She had a passion for shopping and kept a record of how much money she spent on a yearly basis. She spent more money shopping than most people in southern towns made in a year. There were mention of several men friends in the book, but they were never named. They were referred to by their initials. For the last year and a half the only initials that were referred to in the journal were R P. She had met him on a lonely stretch of road one morning as she was coming home from a night out on the town. It was about 6 a m and he had stopped her for speeding. She tugged the seatbelt tightly between her breasts and made sure her dress was high on her thighs. As he approached the car she rolled down the window and asked why he had stopped her. He invited her to the patrol car to see the radar device that showed she was doing 78 in a 55 mph zone.

"I can't believe that I was going that fast, officer." She said, "Is there anything that I can do to convince you that it won't happen again?"

"Just pay the ticket and slow down mam," was his reply. He knew who she was, hell, everyone in three counties knew who she was.

With that she signed the ticket and stomped off towards her car. As she pulled onto the roadway she gave him a wave and was off to the races again.

The next time he stopped her, she had ran a stop sign at the crossroads. He pulled her over again, and the same thing happened, only this time she took her panties off and laid them in the seat beside her before he got to the door. The skirt was a little too short and the wind just happened to be blowing in the right direction for him to see all he needed to see.

"Sure is hot out here today, officer." She said as she opened the door and got out.

"I was just on the way to get a cold glass of tea, want one?"

"Sorry mam, I have another hour of duty before I can socialize." He said as he finished writing the citation for running the stop sign.

"Then why don't you call me at this number when you can." She replied.

A few hours later she got a phone call on her cell

phone asking her to meet him. They met in a little place about 20 miles outside of town, and didn't stay long. They left in his truck and she stayed with him most of the night.

The rest of the journal was mostly documentation of their episodes; dates and times when she would meet "R.P." all of which were because Andrew had meetings with the developers who were interested in getting old man Bryson's land or the board of directors from the main branch of the bank in Knoxville. At one point she went into great detail about her and her "friends" activities but Jonathan skipped most of that chapter.

Along with the stories of their meetings, she mentioned a small file box that was hidden at her house that had some information that could be detrimental to Andrew's career should she ever need it. Strangely enough was the last addition to the journal, the incident of Roger's death. She and he had been out most of the night drinking and had just pulled into the driveway. Roger had wanted to "play around" in the barn for a good old fashioned roll in the hay as he put it and they had nixed the idea of going anywhere else. As they pulled up in front of the garage Andrew had come out from behind the fuel tanks, and brandished a pistol. Before he knew it, he had jerked Roger's door open and held the gun to his head. He took the deputy's government issue Glock from the door panel pocket and pointed it towards his head as he made him get out of the truck. The next thing Diana remembered was the loud noise and the blood spattering on the window. He dragged Roger's body around to the side of the garage, and put him into the open trunk of his car. He told her "get your ass home, we'll deal with this later." She didn't see what transpired next, but she knew she was in for trouble. The last thing she said about the incident was her returning home to wait for Andrew.

"Lots of stuff to digest," Jonathan thought as he packed his bag for the trip back home. They had contacted Andrew at his meeting and told him the bad news. He asked for the body to be returned to Bryson's Grove so the funeral could be performed there.

Jonathan and the sheriff had been on the road for only a short while when he made the comment that Andrew didn't seem very distraught about his wife's untimely death. "Maybe we should put out an all points bulletin for anyone who might find him just in case he tries to disappear." Jonathan said to the sheriff.

"Probably won't be a bad idea," he replied.

Jonathan got on the radio and gave the state dispatcher a description of Andrew's car, a late model Cadillac sedan; not anything like the taste his wife had. It should be traveling west on just about any road that connected from Knoxville to Bryson's Grove.

They settled down for the two-hour drive back to Bryson's Grove. They had just finished discussing their next plan of action in the case when a state trooper called them on the radio. "Car 205 to Investigator Miller," broke the silence over the radio waves. All of the TBI cars had their own radio frequency so they could discuss matters of importance and not let the information be heard by the general trooper population. They also had the regular channels in case they needed to talk to anyone on that frequency. Two years ago, the private investigator's frequency had been installed in the supervisor's cars in case they needed to contact the agents. Jonathan answered the lieutenant's call and was told that Andrew's car had been found at the rest stop just outside of Knoxville. His body was also found outside; behind the vending machine area, which was about 50 yards from the main building. Someone had heard a shot and found his body lying on the ground outside.

"We are just a few miles from there," Jonathan replied, " cordon off the area and don't move anything until we get there. Did you recover a weapon?"

"No we haven't yet, but we are still looking." The trooper replied.

No wonder they couldn't find Roger's weapon, Andrew had kept it with him all of the time.

When they arrived at the rest area, the paramedics had already pronounced him dead. After a close observation of the body and the surrounding area, it wasn't a suicide after all. That is unless Andrew had found a way to shoot himself in the back of the head. The bullet had entered from the lower left side of his head, and he was right handed.

A quick search of the vehicle revealed Andrew's briefcase, a change of clothes in his overnight bag, and a small canvas bag stuffed behind the fold down armrest in the rear seat. When Jonathan opened the bag there was a large amount of cash inside. All wrapped in $10,000.00 packets. After counting the packets, there was $120,000.00 in cash in the bag. No receipts, no paperwork, nothing. Plus, there was no gun found at the scene. He had the identification officers take pictures of the money and the automobile, and they scoured the area to try and find the weapon. There had been no witnesses to the shooting, the only person at the rest area at the time, was a worker inside the building putting up a display for the maps to the mountains. She had heard the gunshot and ran outside. After not finding anything she had just brushed it off to a backfire from a vehicle on the interstate. The next thing she knew was when a trucker had ran inside and told her to call the cops that a body was laying on the ground. He had found the body when he went to the vending machine area for a drink. After some intense questioning they let the driver go and told him that they would be contacting him later in case they needed some more information from him. A couple of K-9 dogs were brought in, but after an intense search of the area, nothing was found. The dogs followed a scent into the parking lot about 50 yards from where the Cadillac was parked, and it ended there.

Jonathan called for the coroner's office and after a while they showed up, just after the wrecker left with the Cadillac. "Looks like the forensic guys in Knoxville are going to have a field day with you," sheriff Thompson said.

"Yea, they probably will, but I'll bet you that the

bullet matches the one we found in Roger. Now the only problem is, where is the damned gun?"

They cleaned up the scene and opened the rest area back up to the general public and headed towards home. Not much was said until they had almost gotten back to Bryson's Grove.

"We've got to find out who the developers are that were working on this land project. That will be the key to the whole thing, I'll bet my boots." The sheriff said.

"I don't know," Jonathan replied. "They wouldn't be involved with this directly; it wasn't a professional hit, I don't think, too wide open of an area and too much of a possibility of being seen from the interstate. No, the person who is responsible for this is covering something up. Besides, I need to get back to Knoxville to follow up on all of this information and get a handle of what is going on."

A short time later, they drove into Bryson's Grove. Everything was in place, although they were sure that everyone had heard, by this time, about Diana and Andrew's deaths. Jonathan let the sheriff out in front of the jail, and decided to go to the restaurant to talk to Sue Ellen before he had to leave. It was getting towards the end of the week and he had lots of things to do, personally and for the investigation. By now his neighbor was probably getting tired of feeding Jonathan's prized pup Poncho, and quite frankly he missed the little fellow. Not that he was really a pup, Jonathan had gotten him a couple of years ago and he had been his constant companion since then. The only times they were apart were when Jonathan had to leave town for an investigation or when he went on a trip on his motorcycle.

The restaurant wasn't very crowded and when Sue Ellen turned around from the cash register, it was kind of hard not to realize that she was glad to see him. He sat down at the counter and said, " got any coffee left?"

"Just one cup, been saving it for just the right person." She said with a gleam in her eye.

"Looks like you guys have been busy the last couple of days." She said. " It is all over the news about the Turner's, and the bank examiners called the bank this afternoon and shut everything down. They are supposed to be here in the morning to do a full audit of the records. What is going on Jonathan? There has never been anything like this happening in this little town."

"I'm not sure Sue Ellen," he replied.

"I have to leave this evening to go back home so I can try to piece the investigation together. There never has been a weapon found, and I am thinking that the same one was used in both murders. By the way, what are you doing this weekend?"

"I really don't have any plans," she said. "Just the usual, I am off work this weekend, for the first time in three weeks. I think the old gal must be feeling sorry for me; why do you ask?

"I have a great little place in Pigeon Forge that I like to visit in the fall, and I thought maybe we could spend some time together and see the colors in the mountains." He said.

" Don't take this the wrong way, Sue Ellen, but I would really like to spend some time with you away from all of this and everything else. I'll get two different rooms at the hotel, or do whatever makes you comfortable, I just want to spend some time alone with you, and get to know you better. I have to leave this evening to go back and would love to meet you somewhere Friday evening or Saturday morning. I would ask you to stay at my house, but I don't want to put you in an awkward position. How about it, will you come?"

"Don't rent the motel rooms just yet," she smiled. "We are both adults and I really don't think you are an ax murderer; besides, I would love to see how a bachelor detective lives. I'll call you when I get off Friday evening, maybe I can talk her into letting me leave a little early. She has been asking me 40 questions about us anyway, and she thinks you are a good man, so who knows, I'll just have to call you."

"Sounds fine to me," he said with a big smile. Here is my cell phone and home numbers, just give me a call when you are leaving and I'll be looking for you."

With that he finished his coffee and walked out the door. As he started his car and pulled out into the street, the sheriff was walking across in front of him. He motioned for him to stop and said, "Just thought you might want to know, both of the bullets are from the same gun." The sheriff said.

"I thought that might be the case," Jonathan replied, "now all we have to do is find the damned gun and who has it. I'm going home, call me if anything else develops; especially if the bank examiners find anything amiss."

"So you have heard about the internal investigation?" the sheriff asked.

"I have heard about most everything since I have been here. I'll keep you up to speed on what I find out from the serial numbers on the money. If the bank examiners find any missing, I'll return it to them; in the meantime, I'm going to have it at the TBI office in Knoxville. Tomorrow is Friday and I plan on leaving a little early. If anything comes up this weekend, leave a message on my cell phone. I am planning on being busy, plus I have two hours to drive and lots of stuff to think about on the way home. This investigation is far from over." He left the sheriff standing in the street. The only thing he wanted to think about for the next few days were a size 7 redhead with a big smile and beautiful green eyes.

Friday was one of the longest days of her life. She took the card out of her apron so many times, that the ink was almost smeared off the back. Not to worry she thought, she had memorized both of the numbers anyway. She had packed her overnight bags after Jonathan had left. Maybe it was wrong, but she was going to Knoxville and have a good time. She deserved it. She had not had a serious relationship with anyone since her husband and she just felt good about Jonathan. Sure, they had snuggled and kissed and touched, but he had been a gentleman about the whole thing. She had longed for him to stay the night with her when they went to dinner, but she knew he wouldn't. He had told her that he didn't want to add anything for the local gossips to advertise, and that he would wait for a time when they would be together for more than one night.

About 2:30 Annie came into the kitchen and told Sue Ellen that she needed to get some fresh air, "go home, take a shower, and get your ass on the road!" she said.

"Don't keep that young man waiting, he is probably pacing the floor right now."

She gave Annie a big hug and left. Annie walked over to the office and made a note on Sue Ellen's time sheet that she left at 6 p m., the usual time. She was just very happy that the young girl had finally met someone that made her smile and inserted the sparkle back into her eyes. It seemed like the shower was taking forever. Thoughts of Jonathan ran through her mind like the wind in the valleys where she had been spending her days off. As she walked through the bedroom, dripping wet from the shower, she could almost smell him in the living room. Not that perfumed commercial smell, you know, the one that all of us have, but is different in fragrance. She opted for jeans and a sweater something that he has said she looked the best in. Although she had never had any children, she had suffered through a weight problem shortly after the trial. Her husband had been so mean to her and made her self esteem drop to such disastrous levels, she forgot about her looks and didn't keep the weight down. When she finally got herself straightened out, she had exercised, dieted, walked, and

Anything else she could do to tighten herself up again. As she stood in front of the mirror, she blushed as she pulled on the red thongs and bra that she had bought herself two years ago. "My present to myself for becoming myself again." She thought as she pulled the sweater over her head. The fire in her hair seemed to brighten with each moment she thought about him. She would muss it up and let it dry naturally.

Fortunately for her she didn't have to mess with it much, it had a natural wave to it that just was very becoming to her. She loaded the bags into the car, and as she turned out of the driveway and on to the street she felt a warm calmness from the depths of her soul. The butterflies had long since been replaced with the excitement of a schoolgirl going out on her first date. As she exited onto the highway and headed east, the sun was just disappearing behind the mountains. She dialed his phone number only to get his answering service. Gosh, his voice was even sexier on the phone. She adjusted herself in the seat, squirming a little, and anticipated the events of the weekend. It would be one that they would never forget, she was almost sure of that.

Jake lit the candles and poured a glass of wine for Charlotte. For the first time in a couple of weeks they finally had gotten to spend an evening alone. He had been away on assignment for a few days, and the bed and breakfast had been completely full for over three weeks.

All of the commotion in town over the deaths of Roger, Andrew, and Diana had pretty much been more than this little town could take. Although it had been only a couple of days, the news had spread like wildfire. It was all over the news and in the paper. The bank examiners had been searching for lost funds, only to find out that Andrew had procured a safety deposit box for himself and didn't have any written records of it. He had taken a box that was supposedly out of order and waiting for a locksmith to repair it and had used it to store a large cache of cash. As the examiners opened the box, they were astonished. There inside the box were several packets of money. All in all when they had finished counting there was $400,000.00 in cash. Also was a small ledger with dates, names, and amounts of money that were given to him from the developers to help with the acquisition of old Mr. Bryson's property. The total of the "consulting fees" were in excess of $650,000.00 the only problem was, there was more money recorded in the ledger than there was in the box. There seemed to be $250,000.00 missing. Of course all of this had been talked about in the bank, and sure enough the head teller, Miss Helen listened to every word. She had a hair appointment that afternoon and after the perm and the conversations with the hairdresser, they had scooped ABC, NBC, and CBS, for the afternoon news.

Jake adjusted the music on the radio and sat the flowers in the middle of the table that he had bought for her. The autumn bouquet smelled ever so good and the aromas blended well with the meal she had prepared.

As they sat down for dinner, the conversations drifted from the recent happenings to what had been going on in their immediate lives. "Anything interesting from your world today?" he asked.

"No, not really" she replied.

"Most of the visitors have left and I can't say that I am sorry that they have gone. This is the busiest season of the year, and although I enjoy the people coming, I am almost glad when they are all gone. Each year we get a little busier and each year there are more and more tourists turned down because of the accommodations, and I am either going to have to make the place bigger, or just quit. Even if it is just the dining room. When they cannot get rooms, they want to make reservations for breakfast, lunch, and dinner. We have a bed and breakfast, not a restaurant. If they want to eat they should go to Annie's!" she said

"Yes, you are right," he agreed,

"But the food isn't near a good at Annie's, and the hospitality isn't either."

"You are just prejudiced," she replied, blushing the whole time.

Jake sure knew which buttons to push when he wanted to. She was almost shy at times, and that is one of the things he loved about her. He gave thanks for the food, their safety, and the many other blessings they enjoyed.

"You know Christmas is coming up and I haven't a clue as to what to get for you." He said.

"Nothing is really needed, I have most everything

I need and lots of stuff that I don't really deserve. I would be satisfied with just spending the time with you here outside of the hustle and bustle of the town." She replied.

"Okay, then we will just have to work on that. I cannot think of any other place I had rather be myself." He said.

"Then it is agreed, we will leave all of the traveling to the others and spend a quiet Christmas here alone. I know there will be visitors from time to time, but at least we will have the peace and quiet. I'll close the business down for a week and we can celebrate as long as we want to." She offered.

Little did she know that it would be a very special occasion too.

After dinner they sat on the couch and attempted to watch a movie. Jake was restless and his surprise was about to get the best of him. As they watched the flames jump in the fireplace he put his arm around her and kissed her softly.

"Charlotte," he started nervously," I love you.

"I have wanted to tell you this for some time. You are wonderful to me, in every way. I just haven't had the courage to tell you. Each time you leave here and go back to town, I long for the next time I see you coming down the driveway. I was afraid that if I did let you know how I felt, that you would be scared away."

She sat there with a sparkle in her eyes, and a confused look on her face. She had thought a lot about hers and Jake's relationship, and there was no doubt in her mind that she loved him, but she never expected this. She hated to leave him when she did, and couldn't wait to get back there either.

"I love you too, my darling. Your soft touch, gentle kisses, and powerful caresses make my body limp when we are together. And yes, it to is hard for me to leave you, but I know I must." She confessed.

"I have been meaning to talk to you about that. I want us to be together always." He said.

With that he reached into the drawer of the sofa table and produced an engagement ring. He knelt on one knee and opened the box.

"I want you to be my wife, if you will have me. I know you love me and you know I love you. I was going to do this in a fancy restaurant somewhere and make it a memorable moment, but I couldn't wait any longer."

With tears of joy in her eyes, she calmly took his face into her hands and rubbed his cheeks with her thumbs.

"I don't know what to say. There is no more romantic place in this world than right here, right now. I wouldn't have it any other way," she said.

As she pulled the blanket away from them they laid on the rug in front of the fireplace. She kissed him softly on the lips and as he wiped the tears from her cheeks, she looked him deeply into his eyes and simply said:

"Yes, my darling. I will be happy to be your wife."

The fire burned slowly down as they lay there in each other's arms talking about all of the things engaged people talk about. Where would they live? What would they do with the two businesses? Or should anything change? It wasn't long before the last embers from the logs were burning in a deserted room. He had picked her up in his arms and gently laid her in the bed. There he had placed a single rose on the pillow next to her. "The first of many," he simply said.

With that she took him into her arms, and thought as they met the heights of their passion that she was in the very place that she needed to be; and that would be where ever he was.

The rays of the morning sun were just peeking through the window when she awoke. She felt his body nestled close to hers, and as she raised her hand to push her hair away, she couldn't help but see the sparkle of her ring in the sunlight. A small smile and a tear appeared, only to be wiped away by his gentle touch, as he turned her face towards his.

"Good Morning my love," he said as he kissed her gently on the lips.

"Good morning." She replied as she threw the covers back. She rolled over and looked him in the eyes.

"Are you sure you want to do this?' she asked.

"Honey if I didn't, I would never have asked you." He replied.

Most of the day was spent with passionate kisses and naked bodies clinging to each other as if there would be no tomorrow.

"We will live each and every day as if it were our last," he said.

Sometime in the middle of the afternoon, they fell asleep in each other's arms.

The next two days, they hardly left the house. There were many decisions to be made. They talked, made notes, agreements, all of the wonderful things two people in love do. They had decided that they should live at his place. They would sell her house in town, but keep the bed and breakfast, of which they finally came up with a name for it. They were sitting on the porch watching the deer and the animals run across the road when all of a sudden out of the clear blue sky came the idea; I think we should call it "Charlotte's Manor." He said. "We have been jokingly calling it that for a long time, and I think we should officially name it that."

"If that will make you happy my darling, then Charlotte's Manor it shall be."

She said as she snuggled closer to him. The afternoon drifted into the evening and they decided to go for a drive in the country. As they rounded the curve toward Preacher's Fork, there was that old buck, chewing his cud and giving Jake that same old stare. As they started to cross the old iron bridge where he found Roger, he didn't say anything for a while. She knew he was troubled, but didn't dare say anything. Ever since that day a couple of weeks ago he had been haunted by the sight of him sitting there in the patrol car.

"I need to tell you something," he said as they rounded the bend in the road towards highway 70.

" I found an old metal box back when I was surveying Mr. Bryson's land some time ago. I read some of the stuff in there, but there was an envelope that I didn't get in to. I just put it in a safe deposit box and almost have tried to forget it. I think I will go into town Monday and see if I can get into the box. Surely the bank will be open, people need to do their business."

They pulled onto the main highway and as she snuggled close to him all she could think of was the wonderful life they would be sharing. She thanked her Maker that He had given her such a wonderful man.

As Sue Ellen turned onto the entrance ramp to Interstate 40 East she picked up her cell phone to make the call. She hadn't much more than opened the flip phone till it rang. Jonathan's voice on the other end was soothing and sensual.

"Hello, just wondering if you had left yet and about where you were." He said.

"I am just turning onto the interstate. " she said,

She could almost see him smiling on the other end of the line.

"Then you should be here just about the time dinner is ready." He replied " I have a small surprise for you. Hope you like beer butt chicken."

"Beer butt chicken, a southern delicacy." She thought. She hadn't had that tasty meal since her brother came home from the Army. It was one of her dad's favorite recipes. You take a half of a can of your choice of beer, stuff it into the butt of a whole chicken, cover the bird with your choice of seasoning, put it on the grill for an hour to an hour and a half and when the wings are up, it is done. The bird absorbs the contents of the can and makes it moist.

"Only if I can make the salad," she said. "I can't let you do all of the work."

"Don't worry, I'll find something for you to do, just get your butt up here, and don't break any speeding laws doing it." He jokingly replied.

Little did he know that she had been doing about 85 mph most of the way.

"Call me back when you get to exit 385 and I'll talk you in from there. You should be there in about an hour." He said.

She agreed to do just that and turned up the radio. As she nestled down into her seat for the drive, she remembered how her dad had taught her how to baste the chicken, the art of greasing up the beer can with bacon grease so it would slide into the chicken easily, and the art of checking it on the grill ever so often. For her dad and her brother it was about every two cans of beer when the chicken would be checked, that is depending on the size of the bird. It was their way of exercising during the cooking process, doing 12-ounce curls.

Thus they would have to have more beer. She smiled and saw them standing outside his house and couldn't wait until Christmas when they would all get together. If Jonathan was still around, maybe she could talk him into making the trip with her. It wasn't that far. Lexington South Carolina was only a half a day's journey and it would be fun.

Jonathan kept a small bag of food open in the garage just so Poncho could get something to eat if he was getting in late. The chicken was cooking, the salad was just about ready, the corn was in the stove, and his special sauce for the chicken was simmering.

About the time he was ready to turn down the sauce, the phone rang,

"How's the dinner going? " she said, "and which way do I turn off of this ramp?"

"You cannot be here already," he said.

"Sure I can and I am, so tell me how to get there." She said with a smile.

Thirty minutes later, after four turns and three stop signs, she pulled into the driveway.

Poncho met her at the car and almost scared her. She wasn't expecting the guard dog to approach her. "Bodyguard, I assume," she asked,

"Yes, the best in the neighborhood. He won't let anyone close to his soup bucket. Give me your bags and I will take them inside. Dinner is almost ready and I have a bottle of wine chilling. How was the trip?" he asked.

"The only problem I had was trying to explain to the state trooper the reason I driving so fast. He didn't say too much until I told him that I was in a hurry to see you, and he just laughed and let me go." She said with a grin.

"I don't need to know anymore, let's go inside. I'll hear about this soon enough." He said. "Oh yea," she said, "I guess the good old boy network works both ways doesn't it? You guys help each other about as much as you rib each other, don't you?"

She playfully swatted him across the rump and gave him a big hug.

"Nice to see you," he said."

"Where do I put my stuff?" she asked. He kissed her softly on the cheek and picked up her bags. As they got to the end of the hallway, he said," my room is on the right and the spare is on the left."

"Then we need to put them in your room, I don't want to have to get up in the middle of the night looking for something to put on in case it gets cold. She kissed him passionately on the lips and said "Jonathan, just be yourself with me. We are both adults, we have wants and needs and we need each other. Let's just have fun and not worry about what happens. We will have a wonderful weekend."

With that he placed the bags at the end of the bed and turned around with a smile.

"I think the chicken is about to fly, we need to go in here and catch it before it gets out the window."

Dinner was more fun than Jonathan has had in a long time. They laughed and talked about mostly everything. After dinner they were washing the dishes and she said, "you know, they make machines that do this and you won't have to."

"I know," he said, "but if I put them in the dishwasher I don't get to stand here and rub up against you." with that she turned around, put her arms around his neck and kissed him passionately. He put his arms around her waist and lifted her onto the table. As he stood there looking into her eyes she smiled and unbuttoned his shirt. He kissed her again and lifted her into his arms. As he carried her down the hallway toward the bedroom, she ran her fingers through his hair and kissed him again. They hastily undressed and found each other under the covers. For the next few hours he gently touched her in places that she never knew she had and made love to her in a way that she had never experienced before. Exhausted, they finally fell asleep. Sometime before morning Poncho came into the bedroom and licked her on the fingertips and woke he up. She slowly got out of bed and opened the back door so he could get out. As she got back into the bed, Jonathan rolled over and snuggled up against her.

When she awoke again, she smelled coffee and bacon and eggs. She found one of his uniform shirts, slipped into it and walked down the hallway. There he stood in his pajama pants and no shirt as she walked up behind him he turned and smiled. "Coffee, tea, or me?" He asked.

"It will have to be coffee first, I don't know if I can take much more of the other." She said with an embarrassed smile. "Jonathan, it has been almost three years since I have been intimate with a man. I thoroughly enjoyed last night, but I will admit, I didn't remember it being that amazing." He turned around and kissed her on the cheek. "Been almost a year and one-half for me. And I will admit that last night was pretty damned amazing for me too. I have always heard that redheads were a passionate brood, but I never knew how much. You are some kind of woman, Sue Ellen. By the way, are you up for a trip to the mountains today? There is a spot before you get into the park that is unbelievable this time of the year. We are about two or three weeks behind you guys with the colors of the leaves, and I think we will be hitting it at the right time. The weather is supposed to be in the high 50's and low 60's and it would be a great day to get the Harley out," he suggested.

"You have a motorcycle?" she asked with excitement.

"Come here and see." With that he walked down the hallway over to the door that leads to the garage. He opened the door and led her into the garage. There in the corner, covered with its own waterproof cover was his pride and joy. As he pulled the cover off her eyes widened with anticipation.

"Have you ever ridden?" he asked.

"No, but I have always wanted to." She said.

"OK, after breakfast we will take a little trip.

The sun was up and shining brightly. He had gotten a leather jacket out of his closet and from the saddlebags he had gotten a pair of leather chaps out. "Try these on and see if they fit. They look like they might just be the right size. She donned the leathers put on a pair of gloves and as he looked at her he told her that she looked like a "natural." As he backed it out of the garage and started it up, the low roar of the exhaust pipes seemed to excite her. "Good thing I brought my boots," she said.

He steadied the motorcycle and she swung her leg over and away they went. He had given her a short lesson in leaning with him as they went through the curves.

Highway 441 is a natural road for a motorcycle.

He seemed like the motorcycle was a part of him as they leaned through the curves. The leaves on the trees were a mixture of colors much like that of a crayon box. She felt an exhilaration that she had never felt before. She leaned forward and said, "Everything looks so different." She had been through here several years ago in an automobile, but nothing looked like it did from the seat of his bike. It didn't take long for him to feel the cushion of her body against his own. For the next few hours they enjoyed the majestic views, the animals in the fields along the road, and the wind in their faces. They stopped for lunch at a little roadside café and there were several other riders with them. When they left there were two other motorcycles that left with them. They had met and talked in the restaurant. Not about anything special, just stuff; about the feel of the freedom of the road, and the feeling that this was the closest thing to flying without wings. Later on in the evening as it had gotten cooler, he started toward home. She gave him a gentle hug as she had positioned her arms around him most of the day. For some reason it had brought back memories of days gone by and another warm body that had enjoyed the same thing.

At sunset, they were almost back to his house. The sun was just going down behind the hills as she leaned forward and whispered into his ear, "thank you for a wonderful day." When they returned to his house, she was almost sad that the day had come to an end.

He made a pot of coffee and as they sat in the den

he asked," well, what did you think about my little piece of heaven?"

"I cannot find the words to describe the feelings I felt today. I have never ridden a motorcycle, and I have to admit that I was scared at first; but you know, after a few miles, I realized what everyone talks about that rides. There is truly nothing like it."

They sat and talked for a long time. She about her past, her troubles with her marriage, and he also about things that he had never talked to another female about.

"I have told you things about me that I have never told anyone else," he said. " I don't know what it is, but I feel really comfortable talking to you. I have to admit that most women make me uncomfortable in this type of situation, but for some reason, you seem different."

They watched TV for a while and soon she was snuggled against him with his arms around her. She turned around and sat in his lap facing him. She slowly removed her sweater and kissed him passionately. They sat entwined in each other's arms for a while and shortly thereafter retired to the shower. They stayed in the shower until it ran cold and they had to get out. They spent another wonderful night together. As the sun rose in the morning and the daylight filled the room, she lay there watching him sleep. He seemed almost childlike. His smiles reflected an almost boyish state. "He must be dreaming," she thought; and she hoped it was dreams of them. As he slept she talked to him. She told him how special she felt when they were together.

It wasn't long after she had given him the last hug

that he woke up with a large smile on his face. She had gotten up and made coffee and was meandering around the house in nothing but a leather vest and a smile. "I am sure Harley Davidson would like to have a picture of that." He said.

She blushed as she turned around, for she didn't know there was anyone else awake in the house. Even Poncho was still in his bed in the living room. As she handed him a cup of coffee, he gently kissed her on the lips.

"When will you have to leave?" he asked

"Right after lunch," she said. "I have some errands to run on the way home, and I have to get ready for work Monday."

"Me too," he said. "I have to get back on this case. I received a phone call from the forensic lab saying they had some information pertinent to the case. I really would like to get this one wrapped up. You know, it is really strange that the surveyor fellow would find two of the three bodies involved in these instances. Do you know anything about him?" he asked.

"He is a native of the area. His parents moved to Florida shortly after he came home from the service, and left him everything in the house. He was a good friend of Mr. Bryson and helped him a lot when he would come home on leave. He is also pretty well connected with Charlotte, the lady who owns the bed and breakfast. Rumor has it that she and he are very romantically attached. It wouldn't surprise me if they wound up being married. She is a nice lady. I have talked with her several times. She too had a bad first marriage and we have had some pretty good conversations about life in general."

"What makes you think they might get married?" he asked.

"Believe me, a woman knows. When another woman has that look in her eyes, you know that it is more than infatuation, besides they are together most of the time. Not in town, but she spends a lot of time at his house, even when he is out working. They are seen in town at seasonal functions, but that is just about it; plus, they look good together, and that says a lot."

"Do we look good together?" he asked.

She blushed again, "I don't know, maybe we need to ask someone sometimes."

"Are you hungry?" he asked

"I could probably use some nourishment, it is a little late for breakfast, how about brunch?" she asked.

"There is a little café a couple of miles from here," he replied, " they make a mean omelet."

"Sounds fine to me, I'll just throw on some jeans and a shirt and will be ready after I smudge on a little make up. Got a ball cap I can borrow?"

"Sure do", he replied. "But you don't have to worry about the make up, you are really beautiful au natural!!"

She gave him a soft kiss on the lips and sent him back into the bedroom to get dressed.

"Do I need to drive?" she asked.

"Naw, I'll get my old beater out of the garage in the back and we can take it. It needs to be run anyway. It doesn't get much use since I have been driving Uncle Sam's chariot home every night." He said.

"Is that just a perk of the job?" she asked

"Not really, I am on call most of the time, and I never know how long I am going to have to stay out or where I will end up." He said.

He put on a pair of jeans and a sweater and walked out the back door. By the time she was ready, he had backed his other pride and joy out of the garage in the back. A bright red 1967 Chevrolet Camero.

"Boy you are full of surprises." She said

"I have had this one since college. I bought it in my senior year and kept it all of this time. I have spent the last two years restoring it to its original state and it has been a lot of fun. I don't drive it much, I am afraid that someone may run into it accidentally or that some of the local thieves may get more attached to it than I do, if that is possible. At any rate, it sure makes me feel good to drive it, especially with a beautiful lady like you to share the ride with." He said.

"I'll bet you say that to all of the girls. You probably cruise the drive inns in Sevierville on Saturday nights and let a different girl ride each weekend." She laughed.

"Not really, you are only the second female that has ridden in this car." He said.

They pulled out into the street and away they went. As they rode through town it was almost like being in a scene from the seventies, she wanted to pinch herself, but was afraid to, she didn't want this dream to end, although she knew that in a few hours she would be on her way back to the real world and prince charming would be back in his. They pulled into the local hamburger stand and as he shut the engine off she said,

"Wonder if they still have roller skates here?"

"I don't know, they haven't in a long time. I haven't done this in years, Sue Ellen, you seem to bring out the teenager in me again." They both laughed and as she put her arm on the back of the seat and kissed him softly on the cheek, she thanked him for a wonderful weekend. As he was ordering the food she tried to remember the last time she had such a wonderful time. It would be very hard to go back to Bryson's Grove and leave this, but she knew the fairytale would soon be over and they would have to resort to using the phone again.

They drove around town for a while, seeing the sites, and even shrugging off a couple of the local "hot rods."

"I'll just bet that if you weren't a police officer that you would take them up on a race, wouldn't you?" she laughed.

"Don't think I haven't considered it, but as sure as I do, the cops would be around the corner and put all of us in jail." He replied.

As they pulled into the garage, he reached over and patted her on the leg; "I sure have enjoyed having you here, will you consider coming back again?"

She gave him a big smile and simply said, "I would love to."

It was getting close to dusk and as he was helping her load the bags into the car she gave him a long passionate kiss.

"You can stay for a while longer if you would like, heck, I would even consider going back with you, just to make sure that you are safe." He told her.

"I don't think that would be a good idea," she said, "we both know that if I don't leave right now that I would not make it back home tonight. I need to be at work tomorrow, Annie can't run the place by herself, and just think of all of the good gossip I would miss out on."

They both laughed, and as she got into the car and shut the door, he pushed in the lock and said for her to be careful and that he would call her as soon as he could.

She pulled out of the driveway and as she was traveling down the street she could see him standing in the driveway; she hadn't felt this way toward anyone since she was in high school, and it was a good feeling. All of the way to the interstate she thought about him and the wonderful way that she he had made her feel.

He walked into the house, and Poncho met him at the door. He hated to see her go, but he knew that he couldn't have it any other way at the present time. He had to finish his investigation and that would take up most of his time until it was done. As he opened his briefcase and sat it on the table, there was an envelope lying on top of the pile of papers that was stuffed inside. Inside it was a card that simply read, "One Free Dinner at Sue Ellen's at your discretion!" He smiled and thought of the sense of humor she had, and that he would definitely take her up on it.

Bryson's Grove was quiet as she pulled into town. It hadn't taken her as quite as long as she thought it would to get home. Of course, remembering all of the wonderful things that had happened to her this weekend played a small part in that too. She never knew that riding a motorcycle could be so much fun; but the one thing that she really couldn't get off of her mind was the wonderful lovemaking sessions that they had enjoyed. His gentle touch and soft passionate kisses were heavenly.

She unloaded the car and got ready for work the next day. She sat down on the couch and thought about him for a long time. She called him to let him know that she had made it home safely, just as he had asked her to. They talked for about two hours and she finally went to bed just before midnight. Every time she closed her eyes she could see his crooked little smile, and it just made her that much more excited about the next time she would see him. The last thing he said to her was that he would come back as soon as he could.

Jake and charlotte had spent most of the weekend preparing and planning for their upcoming nuptials. They knew they wanted a church wedding, but they couldn't decide which one to use. They were both Christians, but neither of them attended church regularly; so they couldn't decide whether to get married in the church, or somewhere else. As they sat on the sofa, making notes, lists, and when to do what lists, she turned to him and said, "When are you going to tell your parents?"

"I am not sure, I thought maybe we might just

fly down there for a few days after Thanksgiving and give them the good news. My mother is going to be pleasantly surprised, and my dad is too. They have been after me for a while to settle down and they really like you. Guess maybe he thought I was going to start sowing my wild oats again."

"I don't think so," she said with a grin. "The only wild thing you are going to be involved with is me!"

They decided to have the ceremony the week after Christmas. It would give them enough time to get everyone notified, and besides Jake's parents always come back to Bryson's Grove for the Christmas Holidays.

"Well, that is everything except the location." She said, "come on Jake, help me with this. We are going to be almost married before we choose a place for it to happen and I am NOT going to have it on the courthouse steps!"

"The steps aren't big enough to hold everyone," he said " and besides the wedding party will have to stand in the street, and that would block traffic, and that would entail us getting a permit to block the street, and I don't think the sheriff would agree to that." She lovingly poked him in the arm, he was kidding and she knew it. That was another of his attributes; he had a great sense of humor.

"How about Charlotte's Manor?" he asked. "On the front porch, there is plenty of room in the yard for all of the guests, it will be high enough that everyone can see with out chairs, and afterwards we can hold the reception inside. It is the perfect place." He said.

"I don't know," she replied. "It will take a lot of decorating and I don't think it would have enough space for the reception."

"We ain't going to invite the whole town, are we?" He asked.

"No, but we need to have enough space for the people we do invite. I don't want everyone to be crowding around inside."

"Ok, then let's think about this, how about we have an open house the night before and have the wedding the next day."

"That won't work, I cannot see you the night before the wedding, and it is bad luck." She said. "You know like something old, something new, something borrowed, and something blue? Is supposed to bring you good luck."

"Want to rent the town hall for the reception?" he asked.

"No silly, I would rather have it here than down there." She said.

"Ok, then let's just have the wedding and the reception here at the house. There is plenty of room to park, there is plenty of room for all of the people to stand, we will do it right here on the front porch."

"And what happens if there is 5 inches of snow on the ground or if it is 23 degrees or something? I can see me traipsing through the snow with my dress dragging a path."

She was about to get frustrated when Jake finally made this suggestion; "let's just use the Methodist church. Brother Baxter would gladly perform the service, it will be big enough to hold all of the people, and then we can have the reception in the basement.

That will eliminate the space problems for the wedding and the reception."

"You know," she replied "that would probably be the best idea. I'll call brother Baxter tomorrow and see if that can be arranged."

"Good idea" he said, "Now can we go to bed? I have to get to work tomorrow; the boss is going to fire me if I don't get to work soon. Not to mention the money it is going to cost to pay for flowers, dresses, spiked punch, etc.!"

"You are the boss, silly and if you spike the punch, I'll buy a chastity belt for the first five weeks!" she joked.

They both laughed and as he turned out the lights he looked at her and asked, "Charlotte, do you want to have any children? We have never talked about it, and if we are, we need to start thinking about it real soon. You are in your early 40's and I am almost 50 and if we do this, we will both be in a nursing home by the time they graduate from college."

"I don't think so, do you? I have lived my life without children so far, and I really don't think that a child would make any difference. If we find that we need something to supplement our time, then we can always adopt one. Lord knows there are plenty of the little fellows out there that need a home, let's just practice making them and decide on that later." As they entered the bedroom she told him that she needed to talk to him about something.

"Jake, are children important to you? If they are, then you might want to rethink this marriage thing. I love you more than anything, but because of a miscarriage I had several years ago, I cannot have any children. I was bout 4 months pregnant and there were complications, and as a result of the surgery, I was told that I could not have any children."

"Charlotte, children are not important to me. If I were twenty years younger, it may be a different story; but at my age, I am thinking about retiring as soon as I can. I get a good pension from the service, I have saved money for years, and made some good investments, and in about 5 or 6 years, I should be able to retire comfortably. I can help you with the bed and breakfast, or just find something else to do. The state has a good pension program also, and I have been contributing to it for the last ten years. I have worked hard all of my life, I would like to enjoy my new life as your husband and try to spend most of my time making you happy. I love you!"

She gave him a big hug, and as he turned out the light she whispered, "thank you my darling, I love you too."

Jonathan dropped his clothes off at the laundry. TBI agents aren't required to wear uniforms for obvious reasons. Most of his attire consisted of khaki pants, dress shirts, and an occasional suit and tie when he went to court. Their cars were unmarked and other than the tell tale antenna on the back, you wouldn't know it from any other vehicle. Ford Motor Company had made lots of money from Government agencies over the years with the Crown Victoria Line of automobiles. They were comfortable, dependable, fast and easy to disguise as the regular everyday automobile. Although the windows were tinted, it still looked like a regular automobile.

As he got to the office, there were the usual cars parked in the usual places. He parked in the usual space, which was as far as he could get from the door. He liked walking. Sometimes for lunch he would take out walking and walk for an hour instead of eating lunch. He had enjoyed jogging earlier in his life, but an old football injury eventually led to surgery and the orthopedic surgeon told him that he would be better off walking instead of pounding his knees. When he got to his office, there was a note for him to call the lab. When he made the call, the examiner told him what he already had thought. Both of the bullets had come from the same gun. Thus the same gun that had been used to murder Pinson was the same one used on Turner. How ironic he thought. Shot by the same gun that he had used to murder Roger. "Karma is a bitch, isn't it?" he thought. But where is the damned thing and who has it now? That would be the key to the whole investigation. But there were some other loose ends too. Like the girl in the park, the unmatched tire tracks that were cast from the evidence of the other vehicle that was at the scene when Jake found Roger's body, and the simple fact that Jake had found both bodies. But there was absolutely no evidence that Jake had anything to do with either one of the deaths. They thought they had found a match to the fingerprint on the beer can that was found near the girl's body, but that proved wrong after more intense tests. As he printed the information from his computer in the car, he thought of the events of the past few days. He could almost see her smiling as he looked into the screen. When the report had finished, he filed it in the folder for the case, and started reading through the information the examiners had put together from their findings. He also took out the diary that Diana Turner had written and read some more in it. There also were the pictures of the traffic accident that claimed her life and the mention of the money and Andrew's dealings with the developers.

The next path of his investigation was to find out who they were and see if they might have gotten tired of giving him money for nothing, as it looked like the development was going nowhere. The permitting process, the approval of the town council, and the bonds needed for a project of this size, was enough to drive anyone crazy. Anyway, he would find what he needed no matter how long it took.

The day drug on as most days do when he is in his office tied down to the paperwork portion of the job. As he looked out the window he thought of Bryson's Grove and the cute little red head that would be giving him a smile when she sat his cup of coffee in front of him, or when she was looking at him as she laid her head on the pillow beside of him.

Sue Ellen walked into the restaurant promptly at 7:00 a m. Annie handed her a copy of the daily menu and told her, "If you don't wipe that grin off of your face, it is going to be awful tired before the evening comes."

Of course there was the usual barrage of questions from her too. Annie and Sue Ellen had become pretty close over the last few months and she had to know what all happened over the weekend. "Spare me the details, I just want to know if you had a good time." She said.

"Wonderful" was all that Sue Ellen could say. She worked most of the day without talking too much. She was still mesmerized by this wonderful man she had been with and hated to leave.

The examiners were still at work when Jake walked into the bank and said that he wanted to get something out of his safe deposit box. After a careful examination of his credentials and the log of how many times he had used the box, they let him in. He retrieved the old metal tin, returned the key to the assistant manager and left the building. He had left the box inside for a long time. Although he had wanted to look in the envelope that had his name on the front of it, he was almost afraid to.

He walked into his office, checked the fax machine, and pushed the play button on the answering machine. Nothing important, just the remnants of a telemarketer trying him to change his long distance service. He put the box on his desk and opted to make a pot of coffee there instead of going to Annie's as usual.

He sat down at the desk, opened the box and removed its contents. The brown manila envelope that had his name on it was sealed with the clasp and tape. He took out his knife and opened the end of it. The document in the envelope was Isaiah Bryson's will.

There had been much talk and speculation about the whereabouts of this document. It had never been found. The only living relative of old man Bryson's was his nephew from out of state, and he had only been around to have the old man deemed incompetent. Hell, he didn't even come back for the funeral. He thought that all was lost when the lawyer told him that because of no documents being found in his safe at home, that all would have to go through probate, and that could take months, even years. As Jake opened the document, there was a letter addressed to him from the old man. It simply read:

"Dear Jake,

I am fighting a losing battle over my land and all of my property. They have been trying to talk me into selling it for some time now. I keep telling them, that I don't need the money, and I don't want this land developed. I worked rally hard all of my life and when my wife passed away I promised her that I would not let anything happen to the farm. In this envelope is the original of my will. I am leaving all of my property to you. There are no living relatives other than my nephew and I have taken care of him with some money that I had put away. Andrew Turner and some developers from Atlanta have been hounding me to death but I wanted you to have everything. You never failed to do anything I asked of you and you always came around even when you were home on leave from the service. This is my way of thanking you for all of the good things you did for Addie and me.

Good luck to you son, and thanks again for everything you did for us.

Isaiah Bryson

Jake sat there in amazement. He opened the other documents and there was a power of attorney for Isaiah's bank account, which was in the First Bank and Trust in Maryville, Tennessee, and a telephone number for the contact person there. He got up and fixed another cup of coffee and as he read on, he found out what had been going on with the Turner's. He told of the incident where he overheard Andrew and Diana talking of the incident with the insurance lady. He talked of the lack of him having his own children and the fact that Jake had always taken care of he and Addie every chance he got. He had often wondered where the lockbox key was from that he found in the old rusty tin that day, but he was sure glad that he had kept it.

He picked up the phone and called the manager of the bank in Maryville, and asked if he could come and see him. The manager said that would be fine and he would be available that afternoon. It was only about 40 miles there and he thought that he might just as well get this over with. Jake never said anything to Charlotte; he just packed the contents of the envelope in his briefcase and headed out the door.

The drive was full of anticipation and mystery. What in the world could the old man have in this box, and why didn't he use the local bank. "Guess he didn't trust old man Turner," he thought as he pulled into the bank parking lot.

The manager welcomed Jake into his office. Jake showed him the contents of the envelope asked him if that was his signature on the notarization of the documents, and the manager said yes. Although the will had never been filed in court, the document was still good, and there shouldn't be anyone to protest it. "Could you open the box for me, or at least go in there with me as a witness?" Jake asked.

"Sure, that is part of my job. Let me get my key." With that the manager walked over to the safe and retrieved the ring of keys that were the duplicates to the lock boxes.

"All of the larger boxes have duplicate keys just so not just anyone could come in here and get into them."

They inserted both keys into the twin locks and turned the keys. The lock clicked and Jake opened the box. Inside there was another book, a diary of some sorts, and old leather bag something like a dentist used to carry. He took out the bag, unsnapped the lock, and opened it up. Inside were packs of money in $5,000.00 wrappers. He and the manager counted the money and when they were through there was $75,000.00 in cash in the bag. Jake couldn't believe his eyes. He had befriended the old man, but he never expected to get anything from him. Most of the townspeople thought Addie would outlive him, but that was to the contrary. The manager suggested to Jake that he buy a cashier's check with the money. He would have to fill out some documents for the federal government if he did, or he could just take the bag and take his chances of getting back home safely with it.

"Can I leave it here for a while till I get all of this figured out?" he asked the manager.

"Sure," he said, it is as safe here as it is anywhere."

"What do I do with the will, do I have to file it in court?" he asked.

"My suggestion would be to take it to your attorney and let him advise you on that. There is going to be some speculations and lots of talk among the townspeople over there, so you might as well go about it the right way from the start. I am sure there will be a hearing and the judge will have to rule the document legal, I know that it is because I notarized it. He had me do it right here in this office."

Jake got back into his pick up truck and headed back to Bryson's Grove. 'Damn that is a lot of money, and what the hell am I going to do with all of that land. There must be 250 or 300 acres in the old man's farm." He never really knew the exact amount of land, but he knew it was big. He and Mr. Bryson would go riding in his old pickup truck sometimes when he would be in on leave, and the old man always had a special place where they liked to go when they had their talks. It was on that very spot that Jake had found the old metal tin, there among some rocks that they had piled up once for a marker on the hill.

The last survey that he had done was on the bottomland. When he got back to Bryson's Grove, he went to the courthouse and searched the tax records for the property. There was a total of 315 acres in the farm. The taxes had been escrowed and the nephew had filed a suit in probate court for the property. Jake was in awe. He didn't have a lawyer, he never needed one. "What am I going to do?" he thought.

At that time he remembered Charlotte saying that she had hired an attorney when she opened the bed and breakfast. He would talk to her about this; he had to tell her anyway.

He walked into the office of the bed and breakfast. "You look like you have seen a ghost," Charlotte said.

"I feel like I have been talking to one. You and I need to talk. Can you leave for a few minutes?" he asked.

They got into Charlotte's car and headed out of town. As the story unfolded, Charlotte could hardly believe what he was telling her. This was incredible. "You know that is the most prime piece of real estate in three counties, don't you?" She said. "There have been developers fighting over that for a long time. There is a virtual goldmine out there for building. The paper mill is planning a major expansion for next year and when it is finished, there will be a lot of jobs available. And you know what that means, more jobs, more people, and they have to have somewhere to live, and there surely isn't enough room in town for them. So they are going to have to build more houses for them."

"I know," Jake said. "I need to talk to an attorney. Do you still have contact with the one you used when you bought the bed and breakfast?"

" Yes, I still have the information; as a matter of fact I started to call him the other day and ask questions about the matters of our businesses and what we should do when we get married. I'll call him tomorrow and ask if we can come in and have a talk with him.

What are you going to do with the money? I guess you had better ask him about that too. You will have to report it to the IRS, wouldn't you?"

"I don't know," he replied. "It is cash, and there wouldn't be any way of tracing it, I could just take a little out at a time whenever I needed it and no one would ever know where it came from. $75,000.00 is a lot of money and I really don't know what to do with it. I don't owe any bills, I pay cash for everything. The building rent is only $200.00 per month, and it wouldn't be that except I agreed to pay Annie that amount just to help with the taxes. I get my pension from the service; I really didn't need to work, now I really don't need to. I could sell the old home place and move over to the Bryson farm, or sell it and.," he thought for a minute. "How would you like to live on the old Bryson place?" he asked. "It has a beautiful old home and we could really fix it up with the money. That would be a job within itself. My parents will never move back here, and we could get a good price for it."

"Let's just leave everything like it is, Jake. We are kind of getting ahead of ourselves here. You know there is going to be a court battle with the nephew and that could take years. I think we just need to go ahead with our original plans of living at your place and move later if we decide to."

She was right, there was no need to rush into anything. There had been enough going on within the last few weeks, and there was no hurry. Besides, no one had lived in the old home place for a while, and it would need some modernizing.

By this time they had come full circle back into town. Charlotte would call the attorney tomorrow morning and set an appointment for them to talk with him about the legalities of the whole matter.

"What's for dinner?" he asked with a grin.

"How about me?" she said.

With that he gave her a big hug and a soft kiss to the cheek and told her that he would see her at the house. As he drove out of town, his mind was rambling. The property has to be worth millions, he thought, especially if it were used for a housing development. As he passed Preacher's Fork there was old "grouchy" nibbling on the trees. He smiled as he passed him up. The old buck didn't move and just looked at Jake as he passed, almost as if he knew he was safe and didn't have to worry about anything. A short time later Charlotte arrived at Jake's house. He was standing in the doorway as she walked up the stairs. "Let me help you with the groceries," he said."

"Thanks, I brought food for a hungry man," she said, " and we are going to eat it when it is finished, and not let it get cold." They both laughed. They had an uncanny habit of cooking a meal only to let it get cold while they made love in various parts of the house.

Dinner was very good. They sat at the table and talked for a long time. She had gotten in touch with the attorney and he had a cancellation for the next day. She booked the appointment because she knew they needed to get to the bottom of it as soon as possible.

The drive to the attorney's office the next day was full of discussions, what if's, and all of the events leading up to the finding of the will. As they entered the attorney's office, Jake felt a little uneasy. The last time he was in a lawyer's office, was to sign his divorce papers, not a comforting thought.

Three and a half hours later they left the office.

The attorney explained to Jake and Charlotte the laws regarding wills, filing them, taxes he would incur as a result of the inheritance he had received, and what he should do about the money. He would draw up the papers for the necessary filings and walk them through the whole process.

The drive back home started in silence. They were both thinking of how this would change their lives. Jake had no idea that this was going to happen. One thing he did know was that the farm would never be developed or sold. A large part of his life had been spent there in good times and bad, and he wouldn't change anything. Or he hadn't planned to anyway. They talked all the rest of the way home making plans for the wedding and what to do with what they had been given. He told Charlotte that he needed her help with all of this and didn't feel he could do it without her.

"I am her for you my darling, good bad or indifferent," she said. "Whatever happens we will endure together."

As they exited off the interstate he squeezed her hand and told her that he loved her, and thanked her for being a major part of his life. As they pulled into town, they stopped at the café for a cup of coffee. Of course the town was still in an uproar over the latest events. They walked into Annie's for a cup of coffee and as they sat down, Sue Ellen came over and sat with them. "How was your weekend?" Charlotte asked.

"Too good to talk about," she said.

"Then I will be expecting juicy details later." They both laughed and with that Sue Ellen walked back to the counter. Sheriff Thompson came in and sat down at the next table.

"Any news?" Jake asked.

"Not much," the sheriff said. "The bank examiners finished their investigation and nothing seems amiss. There isn't any money missing from the bank, and none of the serial numbers from the money in Andrew's car matched any from the reserve that was assigned to the bank. I am guessing that the developers paid the old man off in cash for his "consulting" services, and he tried to hide it from everyone else. I guess they will start working on the nephew now, there isn't anyone else to help them with their acquisition of the property."

"I don't think that will happen," Jake said. "The property will never be sold or developed." With that Jake told the sheriff the story of the will and the money that Mr. Bryson had left to him. They talked for quite a while and Jake told him that he would probably build a house on the farm for he and Charlotte and let the developers find themselves another spot for their housing development.

"What will you do with the old home place?" the sheriff asked.

"I am not sure," Jake replied, "with a few little renovations, we just might have another Charlotte's Manor." With that Charlotte looked at him in amazement. "I am not so sure that wouldn't be a bad idea after all." She said. "I know that you don't want to sell it, and it is in a perfect spot for that very thing." She and Jake finished their coffee and left.

Jonathan called the forensics lab. He had referenced all of the information in the case file and needed some information on the examination of Andrew's car. The technician answered the phone and advised Jonathan that they had found blood samples in the trunk of the car; and after checking them against the DNA from Roger's body, they had found a match. It was apparent that the entries in the journal were correct. Andrew had killed Roger, stuffed his body into his trunk and taken it to the scene where Jake had found it. The only thing was, how did the patrol car get there and who else was involved? Did Diana Turner drive it out there? There was no mention in the journal if she did. Jonathan asked the technician to check the tread patterns from the Cadillac and compare them to the cast that was taken from the scene. A short time later, he called back and confirmed that the patterns matched.

"Ok," he thought. "That clears up everything except how the patrol car got there and the gun. Diana must have driven the car out there, wiped off the prints, and then rode off with Andrew. Now all he had to do was find the gun, figure out who shot Andrew and the case could be closed, or at least be close to complete. He got up from his desk and headed towards the coffee pot. "I have talked to damned near everyone in the south about this," he thought. "But there is a missing link somewhere. Wonder how I can get in touch with the nephew. He was working with Andrew trying to get the property deeded to him so he could get it sold. Wonder if he has anything to do with it?"

He went back into his office and called sheriff Thompson. After a short conversation with the sheriff, he found a telephone number for the nephew and called him. There was no answer, but Jonathan left his name, telephone number, and the reason for the call on his recorder. Working with suspects across state lines was tricky, not to mention inconvenient. If he didn't get any response from the nephew, then he would have to pay him a visit. He made a call to the Pittsburgh Police Department and asked for the homicide detective in charge. After spending at least an hour on the phone with him the detective said for Jonathan to call him the next day if he didn't get a response.

It was getting close to quitting time and he had let his thoughts drift away from the investigation and into a small town diner. "Wonder what she is doing?" He had thought a lot about her since she had left. There were lots of miles between them and even so, he longed to hold her and love her again. He had thought of a million reasons to drive there, but couldn't justify the trip. Besides, there were other things to take care of. Poncho would be waiting on the other side of the fence when he got home and there were laundry and other "honey do" things he had to take care of. As he closed his briefcase and started out the door of his office, the phone rang. It was the detective from Pittsburgh.

"Jonathan, this is Detective Williams, shortly

after we talked, we got a call from one of the nephew's neighbors. She had heard what she thought was a gunshot and dialed 911. When we arrived at the scene we had to break open the door. As we entered the apartment he was laying on the floor of the kitchen with an apparent self inflicted gunshot to the head. There was a note beside the telephone answering machine, and it has some pretty incriminating statements in it. Apparently he was involved in an illegal land deal that ended up going south and felt like he had no where else to turn. There seems to be a banker in your area that was trying to cut him out of the deal and he got mad about it. I'll be back in my office in a little while and will send it to you then." Jonathan thanked him for the information and as he hung up the phone, he leaned back in the chair. He picked up his coffee cup and as he walked towards the kitchen area he thought, "Looks like the final chapter is about to be written in this little story."

The document came across the fax machine about an hour later. Five pages of handwritten information gave him the missing clue to the whole saga. The nephew and Andrew the banker had dreamed up the scam to have Isaiah Bryson deemed incompetent after the old man refused to sell the farm. They were in the process of falsifying some documents and trying to trick him into signing them when the old man died. The nephew had been with Andrew when he shot the deputy and was apparently trying to blackmail him to keep quiet. According to the note, he had met Andrew in Knoxville to pick up the money when the shooting occurred. He had followed Andrew back to the rest area and shot him with Roger Pinson's gun. Andrew had refused to give him any more money until the deal had gone through. And that would be a long time, because the property had to go through probate. Apparently he had kept the gun with him since the shooting of the deputy so it couldn't be recovered and they wouldn't be implicated in the crime. He had driven back home and after a night of drinking and using drugs, he wrote the note and committed suicide.

Jonathan called the detective back and thanked him for the information. They discussed the case for about two hours. The detective verified that the gun that was used was a .40 caliber Glock and verified the serial number. "As soon as you finish with your investigation," Jonathan said, "I need the gun to finish mine. I need to compare the bullet from the nephew to the one's taken from the banker and Deputy Pinson."

"I should be able to send them to you in a couple of days." The detective replied. "The coroner has the body now and I'll forward his report to you as soon as it is ready."

"That will be good," Jonathan told him. "If you don't mind, send them to me via electronic mail and that way I won't have to wait on them here. I need to go back to Bryson's Grove and go over all of this with the local authorities so they can close their investigation. As a matter of fact, just forward the package with the gun and the bullet to my attention at the Sheriffs Office in

Bryson's Grove. I should be there in the next couple of days, and thanks for all of your help." The drive home was one of relief. He had been engrossed in this case and not much else except Sue Ellen from the beginning. When he got home Poncho was dancing a jig. He knew it was long past time for his master to be home and he was wagging his tail and jumping for joy. As he entered the house he sat his briefcase on the kitchen table and reached for the phone. She would be home by now and maybe they could talk for a while. He longed to hear her voice. The smooth tone of her voice and her gentle laugh was something that soothed him, especially after a hard day's work. His thoughts were running rampant and as he entered the bedroom to put his gun in the bedside drawer, she answered. "I am not interested in buying tickets to the policeman's ball, but I would be interested in being frisked by a certain TBI agent. I have been a bad girl and you may even have to put the cuffs on me!" He laughed aloud. "Hello to you too. I almost thought I had gotten a new-recorded message on your phone.

It is good to hear your voice, I have missed you." He said with a grin.

"I missed you too, Jonathan. You must have been really busy for the last couple of days. I have kept you a piece of Annie's apple pie but if you don't get here soon, it will be moldy." She laughed.

"I will be there tomorrow or the next day, don't get rid of the pie, or just make me a fresh one. I need to check with Charlotte and see if there are any rooms available. I have gotten some information that has broken the case, and I need to come back to finish it up."

"Is that the only reason you have to come back? " she teased.

"No there is a certain red head that is the suspect in another case and I need to interview her extensively." He said with a grin.

They talked for quite a while. She had asked about the case, but he reminded her that he couldn't tell her anything until it was completely finished, and that then he could only tell her what he would be able to tell the local news authorities. There were some pretty personal items involved in this case. Diana Turner's Journal would be considered evidence, the note from the nephew implicating all who were involved, would be also; and besides all of this was personal information and because of the new privacy laws, this information had to be sealed. He promised to see her in a couple of days and they would make plans to spend some time together. About midnight she softly wished him a good night and they ended their conversation. He lay there for a long time. Many thoughts were running through his mind. Little did he know that a couple of hours away, there was someone lying awake in the bed having some of the same thoughts. As she rolled over and hugged her pillow, she remembered the last time she was with him, and how nice it would be to be near him again.

The drive to Bryson' Grove proved to be just what he thought. The closer he got the anticipation of seeing her again grew greater and greater. As he arrived at the sheriff's office, sheriff Thompson was waiting on him. He had called him on the way and filled him in on the latest developments. As he walked into the office the sheriff offered a cup of coffee and they sat down. For the next three hours they went through the case step by step. The detective had overnighted the package with the gun and the bullet from the nephew. The serial number on the gun matched the records from the sheriffs' office and Jonathan told the sheriff that he would take it back to the crime lab in Knoxville and confirm the match of the bullets and the rifling from the barrel of the gun. Jonathan stayed at the sheriffs' office until quitting time for Sue Ellen. As she walked out the door of the restaurant, there he stood beside his car. "Need a lift home?" he asked.

"No, I am not allowed to ride in a government automobile; but I do need an escort. You know how dangerous it is in these parts." She laughed. With that she walked to her car and he followed her home. "Are you hungry?" she asked.

"Only for you my darling." He replied. He took off his gun, laid it on the table, and slowly walked towards her. He took her in his arms and gave her a long passionate kiss. As they made their way to the bedroom she could barely believe he was there. They took a long hot shower and made love for the better part of the night. As he lay there looking at the moonlight shining on her hair, his mind was racing in many different directions. He didn't know where they would end up, but the one thing he did know was that he was right where he wanted to be. He had some plans to discuss with her, and he hoped she would be receptive to them. Not to far away outside of town, the moonlight was shining on someone else who was also making plans. It wouldn't be too long before wedding bells would be ringing. Tomorrow would be another day in town. The story would come out in the newspaper soon and some of "The Secrets of Bryson's Grove" would be revealed.

The End

www.ingramcontent.com/pod-product-compliance
Lightning Source LLC
Chambersburg PA
CBHW030146010826

48973CB00002B/751